I0562004

Love, Life, and Logic

Uday Mukerji

Harvard Square Editions
New York
2016

Love, Life, and Logic

Copyright © 2016 Uday Mukerji

Cover painting by Antoinettew ©

None of the material contained herein may be
reproduced or stored without permission of the
author under International and Pan-American
Copyright Conventions.

ISBN 978-1-941861-26-4
Printed in the United States of America

Published in the United States by
Harvard Square Editions
www.harvardsquareeditions.org

*This book is a work of fiction. References to real people,
events, establishments, organizations, or locales are
intended only to provide a sense of authenticity, and are
used fictitiously. All other characters, and all incidents
and dialogue, are drawn from the author's imagination
and are not to be construed as real.*

Chapter 1

"LISTEN TO ME; I'm a big girl. I know what I'm doing." Adeline paused. Her deep blue eyes looked straight into mine. She didn't even blink. There wasn't a shred of doubt in her voice; if anything, she was calm, composed, and confident. "Don't read too much into it. Just live it as long as it lasts."

As much as I wanted to do just that, my conscience failed to keep up. I looked at her, all confused. Truth be told, I was still recuperating from the aftershock of waking up to her lingering perfume in my bed and the sound of pots and pans banging in the kitchen.

"Coffee? . . . Here you go." Adeline handed me a mug, and sprinkled black pepper and cheddar cheese into a bowl. She was standing behind the kitchen counter, wearing one of my white shirts; she must've pulled it out from the closet. The unbuttoned shirt covered her arms and part of her upper thighs, revealing every curve of her nicely toned body and long legs as she moved around. An electric shock passed through my body; I stood there numb. I noticed her hair had a beautiful bounce and a natural, gorgeous shine, but the carefree morning had displaced some of the unruly bangs over her eyes. She quickly ran her fingers through her hair and flipped it back.

I couldn't deny that Ade looked amazing standing there wearing close to nothing. That careless beauty didn't need any help from Maybelline or L'Oréal. I had never felt such overwhelming attraction, but I knew I couldn't possibly indulge again. She was too young. It was insane. I had to restrain myself. I lowered my eyes and silently sipped my coffee.

Still, there was no denying the fact that she was, indeed, a big girl.

I tried to put the pieces together from the previous night, but nothing appeared clear. My eyes were burning. I couldn't remember a thing—when or how I had gotten home. I thanked god for bringing me back to my bed.

Adeline was still standing in front of me, holding a glass bowl and gently beating a few eggs in it. I couldn't help staring at her. As reality started to sink in, my mouth dried up, and my head started spinning. I heard myself blurt out, "Oh, no!"

"*Was?*" I guess her native German came out in utter confusion. She immediately apologized and corrected herself, "What? Don't you like scrambled eggs? You don't really have a lot of choices here, you know. I didn't have many options."

"No, it's not about the scrambled eggs; that, indeed, is a great choice." I wanted to reassure her; but I still couldn't get my head around my half-naked, next-door neighbor so freely roaming my kitchen with a bowl in her hand. How did that happen?

Adeline looked impatient; maybe, my long, awkward silence had something to do with it. She quickly changed track. "I thought you could at least spoil me today. After all, it's my birthday. You remember, right?"

I had totally forgotten. How could I ignore her on a birthday? I immediately apologized and wished her happy birthday with a warm kiss.

And that, I soon realized, was possibly my second mistake. There was no way I could indulge in a relationship now; and I couldn't take it back, either.

"I thought that'd never come." Ade rubbed in more guilt.

"I'm sorry. What do you want to do today?" I tried to divert her attention.

"You decide. It's your gift, right?"

"Well, how about a good brunch to start with? Are you hungry?"

"I'm famished. Otherwise, what do you think I'm doing in the kitchen?"

Ade immediately put down the bowl and went to the bedroom to pick up her clothes from the floor, but she gave up halfway. "Forget it—I'll get it later. See you in half an hour?" She picked up her shoes, buttoned her shirt, and walked out the door, shoes dangling in her hand.

I was still dazed; but I had to shave and get ready quickly, so I headed for the bathroom. I stood there motionless under the shower for quite some time, listening to the water gushing down the drain. As the hot shower worked its magic and relaxed my muscles, I clearly remembered how I ended up with Adeline last night. At a normal pace, the series of events that had unfolded in the past eighteen hours could easily take days or months; I hadn't expected any of this to happen, especially after what I had left behind in Singapore.

Yesterday evening, when I had first heard someone knocking at the door, I thought it was rather odd. I wasn't expecting anybody; in fact, I didn't know anyone there, except my two neighbors I met in the elevator: a couple of German girls in their early twenties, studying medicine at the Medical University of Vienna and working part-time in a local hospital. When I first ran into Catherine two days before on my way to lunch, and Adeline, the very next day as I was coming from my jog, I had no idea how disruptive an innocent 'hello' could be.

I answered the door and was more than a little surprised to see Adeline again. She had Catherine and a new girl with her, possibly another roommate, I thought.

Before I could say anything, Adeline asked, "Aren't you inviting us in?"

"Sure, come on—"

But she didn't even wait for me to finish. She was already in.

I took a step back, more overwhelmed than puzzled. What was she, a child? How could anyone walk into a mere acquaintance's house like that? However, before I could ask anything, she introduced her roommate, Gigi; and she put her arm around Cat, "You've already met this girl, right?"

I looked at Gigi and shook hands with her, "Hi! I'm Rohan Fernandez."

"I guessed as much," she replied. "I heard you're from Singapore, right?"

"But I'm originally from India."

"You don't quite look like an Indian, though. You're tall, and have a fair complexion; and you don't have any Indian accent either. If you don't believe me, come I'll introduce you to an Indian IT guy in our hospital." Gigi sounded sincere.

"Well, my dad was half-Portuguese, my mother is Indian, and I was born in India. That's as much Indian as you get." I just wanted to be left alone, and here I was laying out my entire birth history in front of three perfect strangers.

Possibly, there was a sense of unhappiness in my voice. Cat was quick to apologize. "We're sorry to barge in and disturb you like this."

"No, we aren't." Ade jumped in and pulled her away. She looked me directly in the eye and said, "We've an invitation for you, handsome."

"Ha-ha, very funny! Invitation to what and where?"

"You'll see. Why do you want to know every detail like a woman? Don't you even feel a little tempted to go out with three beautiful girls on a Saturday evening? Or would you rather be bored in your apartment? Come on, get dressed; we're going to have dinner first, and then, we're going to party at our colleague's place."

I felt as if Cat was about to say something, but Ade stopped her. Then she looked at me and said, "See you at seven," and quickly dragged her roommates out the door.

I wasn't sure what to make of all that had happened in those five minutes, but Ade hadn't given me any time to think. I told myself that having some company in a foreign country couldn't be that bad. Since I had left Singapore six days before,

I had barely spoken with another soul, let alone had dinner with others. I was in complete mess. I missed my son, Matthew and daughter, Lisa. That day, I simply emptied my heart and walked out. I had been spending last few days ruminating over all these and my failed relationship with my Chinese Singaporean ex-wife – Mimi. But that had to stop. Now that my old world had crumbled, I needed to mingle and make new friends again. Besides, what better place to meet people, exchange ideas, and get a fresh perspective on life than Europe?

I could always back out after dinner I thought.

As instructed by Ade, about an hour and a half later, we reconvened at the lobby. As they came one by one through the door, I could hardly recognize them. What women do in front of a mirror with few brushes and colors is, indeed, an art; they transform themselves and their personalities into their chosen characters. Ade had turned herself into a party girl for the night; her short black dress and high heels had definitely accentuated her long legs. I figured she'd be at least five seven. She looked all set to dance the night away. I must say it was quite a transformation from what I had seen earlier that evening—in torn jeans and a cotton tee. But I also knew that not everything in life is really the way it appeared.

"Where are we going for dinner?" I asked.

"Are you in a mood for Mediterranean?" It looked like Ade was in charge of the evening.

"Sure, why not?" I also felt a little adventurous, though my excitement had nothing to do with the food; I hadn't had an unplanned evening like this in a long time. Up until a few days before, my life had been as routine as traffic lights; I was curious to see what a deviation could bring.

We all walked to a small Greek restaurant a couple of blocks away from the apartment building. Although I had explored the area a little over the last few days, I'd had no idea that a restaurant like this existed in our neighborhood. I must've missed these exact turns; after all, all roads in that neighborhood pretty much looked alike, with mostly prewar houses standing in rows and tram tracks twisting and turning through the lanes and alleys.

The restaurant was smallish, with eight tables inside and two on the patio. However, the beautiful white lacy drapes and mahogany furniture gave it an expensive feel. Servers looked professional in pressed uniforms. Greek copper and bronze artifacts adorned the walls. The tables had low-hanging lights overhead, with lampshades made of stained glass in copper frames; they seemed authentic Greek, and I wondered whether the owner had flown them in from Greece.

As soon as the wine was served, Ade stood up. "What're we drinking to?"

Cat raised her glass and suggested, "To new friends?"

"Yeah, that, too." It was obvious that Ade had something else in mind. We all looked at her, but she didn't explain. Instead, she announced, "But first, to tonight. We aren't going home until we're happy, right?"

Everybody cheered, but I shivered a little inside. Was this a mistake? I was already looking for my exit strategy. I was definitely not in the mood for a wild night out; though I was beginning to realize taking off wouldn't be easy.

With Ade around, there was no way we would ever run out of conversation; she had this amazing ability to entertain others, even if it came at her own expense. She joked about her uneven eyebrows, not that I could find any difference, and then her mounting credit card bills. She said, "They trap me into buying things I can't afford, then they tell me not to worry—I can always pay later and buy more now. And get this, they love clients like me more than they like you"—she pointed at me—"because I can't pay up in full at the end of the month. So, they charge exorbitant interest like loan sharks to poor people like us. Disgusting, right?"

Suddenly Cat jumped in and said, "Who're you calling poor? Your father is rich."

"My father isn't rich," Ade protested. "Rich people have islands and jets, and they'll still be left with enough, even after taking ten trips to the moon. And so what if he's rich? That money has nothing to do with me. I didn't earn it."

I was quite surprised by Ade's indifference to her family's wealth. I thought she could've easily avoided working regular night shifts if she had accepted a little help from her father. But maybe she preferred total independence from her family.

We were having so much fun that, looking at us, nobody would've believed that I had not known any of the girls three hours before. With delicious food, wine, and great company I didn't even notice how quickly time passed. I felt alive; and more surprisingly, I found comfort and peace among unfamiliar faces. I guess, I was slowly settling in.

Cat and Gigi had been texting nonstop for about last half an hour. I thought nothing of it until a black BMW pulled up on the street and both Cat and Gigi stood up. "Well, see you guys at eleven?" Ade asked.

Gigi said, "Sure." They both turned to me and said, "Later," and quickly jumped into the car.

I didn't have any time to ask questions; I was a silent spectator in an action-packed scene. I looked at Ade, and then at the empty street, and back to Ade, trying to figure out what had happened.

From my bewildered face, Ade must've thought she owed me an explanation. "Don't worry. They'll join us at Michelle's place. That guy in the driver's seat is Jake—Cat's boyfriend. And anyway, am I such bad company?"

"Of course not," I said; but I also couldn't help thinking, so much for my exit plans. Suddenly I felt separated from her by a thick wall of my own thoughts. I was fuming inside. I didn't want to look at her. Most certainly I couldn't leave her all alone there. I felt trapped; now I couldn't leave even if I wanted to. Why didn't she tell me the whole plan?

Ade noticed my indifference. "What's wrong? I lost you for a while."

My eyes were still fixed on the narrow, deserted road. As the darkness fell on another summer evening, Vienna started to light up. The cathedrals and museums aren't the only reminders of a glorious past here, history seeps through everything. The Victorian street lamps, the cobbled road in front, and the age-old houses all around calmed me down pretty soon with their ancient serenity.

I knew it was partly my fault. I had too much going on in my head. Obviously, I wasn't ready for such social gatherings yet. I simply wanted to go home, delve into the situation I was in, and work out a peaceful transition in my mind. I was tired of being angry all the time. If you think separation or divorce is strenuous, try dancing around the issue; that's totally exhausting. And I guess Mimi and I had been doing that for a long time.

I quickly snapped out of my thoughts and apologized. "I'm sorry. I was thinking of something else."

"Please don't be. I should apologize to you instead. I literally dragged you out on a Saturday night; I didn't even ask whether you had plans already. I was wrong, and I'm sorry."

I felt her sadness and remorse were genuine. Her usual exuberance had disappeared, her face turned pale and the light went out of her eyes. I immediately felt terrible; I had no intention to hurt her feelings. Hadn't I hurt enough people already? I was desperate to salvage the situation. "And thank you for that; you saved me. I had nothing else to do anyway." I pulled my chair closer to the table and looked directly into her eyes.

She kept quiet; I thought she was processing what I had said, but I wanted to steer the conversation in another direction. I asked, "What's the plan now?"

Ade shrugged, but smiled a little. "Whatever you want."

"How about another drink?"

"Sure. I would like that."

Soon she looked much more relaxed; she flipped her hair back and started pulling at her pearl necklace as if it was fitted with an elastic cord. Then suddenly she leaned toward me and asked, "I don't know anything about you. Tell me, what're you doing in Vienna?"

I wasn't sure where to start; I wasn't sure myself why, of all places, I had come there. After Mimi and I had signed the papers about six days before, I applied for a long leave and simply took off. At that point it could've been any place; the destination wasn't important. I simply wanted to get out of Singapore for a while. And before I knew it, I was on a flight to Vienna. I guess, my dad's sudden death about four months before had something to do with it. Last year, he went there to attend a conference and he loved it; he never stopped talking about that place ever since.

My marriage had ended long before the closing ceremony took place. After a couple of years together, I had realized that I had morphed into someone new. Right or wrong, I didn't know; but my life looked shallower by the day. I often stood in front of the long mirror in our bathroom, looking for the old Rohan, but that fellow was long gone, leaving behind a shell— one that had started to grow a couple of gray hairs here and there and had developed a slightly bulging stomach.

I wasn't sure when and where I lost that old Rohan. However, every now and then, whenever I got a glimpse of him, hundreds of unsettled questions from my childhood came prodding my memory.

There're always layers upon layers of hidden feelings and emotions in every human head. Physics, chemistry, history, and geography classes had taught us that there's always more than what we can see; to unravel those mysteries, we have to ask questions. Life lessons are no different. I knew the part of my life I could see was only the tip of it; I had to keep peeling those layers. The problem was that I'd stopped asking questions after my marriage to Mimi. Was that to escape the hard truths in life, or to avoid confrontation? I didn't have an answer. All I could think of was to stop doing what I had been doing for years. Consequently, I left everything in the hope of wiping clean my last twelve years of relationship with Mimi; I wanted to start searching underneath all those layers to find the purpose in my life.

Mimi and I had always had our share of problems. But what marriage doesn't? It doesn't make everyone leave home. Did my quest for answers provoke me to end the marriage? Or had my marriage failed and left a void, and my thoughts slowly crept in to occupy that space?

I didn't know; I wanted to find that out too. I looked at Adeline and tried to articulate myself. Her gaze was still fixed on me, waiting for an answer. I could tell her about my childhood confusions, my somewhat unfulfilling career choice, my now-meaningless ambitions, and my failed marriage, or about my quest to find a connection to the rest of the world. The difficulty was that I had no idea where all that was leading to. How could I explain all this to a twenty-three-year-old girl? There's a time and place for everything, and I didn't want to spoil her perfect evening with a complicated divorce drama. I politely said, "It's a long story."

"We have time," she replied calmly, and pulled her chair closer to the table.

I was left with no choice. Still, I decided to keep my personal life as far as possible. I didn't want her to feel sorry for me; I was sad all right, but I wasn't so sure whether I myself felt sorry about my decision.

So, I asked, "Did you ever wonder what our purpose in life is? I know there's definitely more to it than what's visible—something beyond chasing our personal dreams. There must be a connection between each of us and eternity. A dream job, a nice car, a happy family are all good; but they don't explain the purpose of our being here, being alive, do they?"

Adeline was listening to me attentively; her eyes were wide open, but obviously she wasn't so sure what this had to do with my trip to Vienna. After a while, she said, "No, they don't. But could you please elaborate?"

Indeed, I wanted to; I was dying to talk to someone. I had spent a great deal of time thinking how most people's lives are the same; and yet no two people's lives are ever alike. Most of us go to school when we're young, we get a job, maybe fall in love, sometimes have kids, and grow old; and then, one day we all die. But when we take a closer look we find out that in spite of all these similarities, our lives are all too different. So what is that one thing that links us all together? There must be something beneath the surface; but I still didn't know what that was and how I could ever find it.

I decided to keep my answer as simple as I could. I told Ade, "All I know is this: Each of us is like a single letter of the alphabet; most of us don't make much sense individually. But when these letters are put into words, and then, words into sentences, they make more and more sense. And these sentences eventually become brilliant poems, heartbreaking stories, and intense speeches, giving a whole new dimension to those individual letters. I'm talking about finding that kind of link to eternity, something that helps any human life feel connected—and more meaningful than someone's personal aspirations and goals." I paused. "I'm not making any sense; Am I?"

"Of course, you do, though I never really thought about life that way. Please. Go on." She picked up her wine glass to take another sip, but I noticed there was nothing left.

I quickly reached for the wine bottle on the table and refilled her glass. "So what I need is to find that link, and my purpose in life, before it's all over." I looked her in the eye and added, "Now enough about me. Tell me what you make of life." I didn't want to keep going on and on about my deep-seated dilemmas. In fact, I started to feel a little uncomfortable; I had never shared these thoughts with anyone. All I had till that point of time were hundreds of questions, and no answers.

But Ade said, "Wow! That's deep. To me, life is simple, and it's made of all the small pieces of a big jigsaw puzzle; each life has one complete picture, but guess what, you can't see the full picture in the beginning. All we're doing is playing the game, trying to fit our pieces next to each other. Of course, at times we put in the wrong pieces, and when we realize that, we have to take them out and replace them with the right ones."

I was stunned. I had no idea that behind her bubbly, vivacious exterior were such crystallized thoughts about life.

Ade told me that she had decided to be a doctor at a very early age since her mother died of colon cancer when she was only twelve. Frequent trips to hospital those days had opened her eyes, and taught her a great lesson: there's possibly nothing more rewarding than being able to cure and relieve people of pain and suffering. Although she always wanted to make herself useful in the society, she didn't think even for a day that she would play any role in changing the world. She quietly wanted to solve her own jigsaw puzzle. To her, it was a lifetime's work. I looked at her with genuine curiosity. She continued, "And since I don't have access to the full picture first, I make a lot of mistakes along the way; and I have to do it all over again. Take my ex-boyfriend Alex, for example. I thought he was the one. But turned out that I was wrong again."

I didn't ask her to elaborate, because those memories are usually sensitive and painful. And that gesture really seemed to touch Ade. Her eyes became slightly moist; was that gratitude, or was she feeling her old pain all over again? I kept quiet and wondered which was her true self. Was she a deep-thinking, radical socialist or was she like any other twenty-three year old girl, with the usual dreams and aspirations in life? Maybe she was still trying to figure that out, like most of us with contradictions and dilemmas.

We both kept quiet for the next few minutes; then at the sound of a text message on her phone, Ade jumped up. "We gotta go; they're gonna kill us for being late." Indeed, we had completely lost track of time. Since Cat and Gigi had left, we must've spent more than two hours talking, yet it felt like few minutes. I smiled and she smiled back as we prepared to leave. Now that I understood Ade better, I didn't feel so reluctant to go to the party after all.

When Ade and I appeared on Michelle's doorstep, it was past midnight. The party had already gathered momentum; the apartment was teeming with people. Usually nobody notices who is coming and going at that point, but as Ade entered the room, everything stood still. Everybody started singing, "Happy birthday to you!"

I was taken aback; I had spent a whole evening with her and had no idea that it was her birthday. Immediately I pulled her aside. "Why didn't you tell me it was your birthday?"

"It wasn't," Ade replied calmly.

"So what's all this?"

"It wasn't my birthday then; now it is." The mischief in her eyes led me to the clock.

Suddenly an emotional awakening consumed my body and mind. I felt an overwhelming urge to kiss her, and I leaned forward . . . but suddenly Cat came from nowhere and pulled her away, 'Just borrowing her for a minute.' They disappeared into the dining room.

I stood there, thanking god for saving me from making a serious mistake. What was I thinking? I still had so many issues to figure out; my head was like a Dumpster. There was no space to indulge in more complications.

But Ade came back in a couple of minutes. She put herself in the same position—against the wall exactly as she stood there before Cat whisked her away. "Sorry about that," she said. "I'm ready now."

"Ready for what?" I asked nervously. It was obvious from her naughty smile and half-closed eyes that she wanted a total replay. I was embarrassed. It was a spur-of-the-moment thing; I didn't know how I could explain to Ade that it would never work. I was thirty-six, divorced with two kids, and Ade was barely twenty-three. Besides, priorities in life are very different at early twenties and after mid-thirties. I didn't want to lead her on if I couldn't follow through.

But to Ade, nothing seemed to matter; clearly she simply wanted to try her jigsaw pieces. She grabbed my neck tightly with both her arms, pulled me toward her, and kissed me. Needless to say, I kissed her back, and I felt something I hadn't experienced for ages; I felt alive.

The crowd cheered, "Go girl, go!"

Ade declared, "I just claimed my birthday present," and walking past the crowd, dragged me to a quieter place in the balcony to take care of unfinished business. The rest of the night passed like a runaway train—raising all the red flags, leaving behind everything and everyone familiar, destined to crash into pieces, to be picked up later.

The sound of my cell phone finally brought me back to my senses. I had no idea how long I had been standing under the shower—maybe ten, maybe twenty minutes—feeling the tepid water falling gently over me, caressing my feelings. Absolute calmness gripped my body and mind; however, I had a feeling that it was more like the stillness before a tornado, or the lull before a calamity.

When a storm breaks out in the mind, it can be more catastrophic than one on the outside. We can, at least, estimate the power of the wind in a coming storm, and try to take precautions. However, we are yet to determine the speed of the mind; so can we really fathom the extent of the devastation if a storm breaks out in our head? If we lose our houses to a hurricane, we can rebuild more, and if we lose our roads, we can construct new ones; but how often have we heard of anyone being able to rebuild or reconstruct a mind?

The phone was still ringing. I rushed out of the shower, and picked it up, just as it went silent. It was Ade. But instead of calling back, I decided to get dressed and go see her myself. I was trying to keep calm till the strong wind passed me by; the whirlwind was so close that running wasn't an option. I took a hard look at the powerful tornado swirling around me. I knew that if I survived the calamity, I would be thrown miles from here. One by one, the faces of my ex-wife, Mimi, my son, Matthew, and my daughter, Lisa, appeared before me, and I was trying to hold on to them tightly. But the swirling wind was pulling them away, and I was slowly losing my grip.

Maybe I should've stopped the relationship right there, but there was a thrill and excitement in the rushing wind. I felt intoxicated and powerless. After a while, I stopped fighting myself and decided to go along wherever the wind took me.

Chapter 2

THE WHIRLWIND, indeed, swept me six hundred miles away from Vienna. Five days later, I woke up in Lauterbrunnen, a quaint little village in the Swiss Alps. The last few days passed me by in a trance. Intense love and desire had consumed my body and mind. But I quickly realized that I was getting hooked all over again, and I was losing sight of my goal—my search for the truth behind this charade we call life. So, I immediately pulled out, and left Vienna.

School, career, and family: maybe they're all as important in life as breathing. But isn't living more than breathing in and out? At any given moment, seven billion people are taking in oxygen and breathing out carbon dioxide; and see our atmosphere isn't yet filled with carbon dioxide. And why is that? Fortunately, plants and trees are doing exactly the opposite to replenish the continuous supply of oxygen. Is that a sheer coincidence or is there any connection between the two complementary processes? I always thought everything around me was connected with an invisible thread like a fishing line. And I needed to find that connection. I definitely didn't have time for another relationship.

All I wanted was to get my mind back on track. I was beginning to like her too much; and I didn't like that. I had no time for frivolous relationships. I knew I certainly owed an explanation to everyone there: Adeline, Cat, Gigi and to all their friends for my sudden Vienna exit; but I couldn't get to that until I was able to see things in perspective again.

At Lauterbrunnen, everything was at peace: the cliffs, the falls, the snow on the mountaintops at a distance, the trees, even the people living there. The summer was in full bloom; colorful flowerpots in balconies were vying for attention. Lush green carpet covered the mountain slopes. Bright sunlight piercing through tall trees reflected on shiny leaves from in-between the shadows. I admired the tranquility which suggested total harmony between nature and mankind. Such places make you realize that silence doesn't mean no activity; it means highly synchronized actions, much like the work of a well-tuned motor. More noise and vibration never assure better engine performance; indeed, quite the opposite.

At Lauterbrunnen there was no morning rush or traffic pandemonium. Moreover, there was no fighting going on inside my head. Each person there decided their own pace; and that person alone would decide whether they wanted to climb uphill or go downhill. I knew that eventually I too had to decide; I couldn't stay in bed forever. But at that point in time I had no clue what to do next.

Still lying in bed, I leaned back against the headrest and noticed the snow-capped peaks through the wide glass window in my room. For fraction of a second, I missed the scent of Ade's chilled lavender perfume like a new amputee misses their leg the first time they awake in a hospital bed. I had become addicted to that scent over the past few days; but today I didn't want to come face-to-face with any of that. Maybe someday, when my bruises had healed and my mind would be more at peace. After all, everything heals with time.

It's true that the human body and mind are so created that everything takes care of itself. When someone breaks their arm or leg, the bones heal on their own; the cast only helps to hold them steady in one position. Similarly, ointment relieves a person from the pain of a cut, but it doesn't rejoin the two ends of the skin. I knew that my mind would heal on its own. All I needed was to hold it steady for now.

But that was the difficulty. Holding my mind steady? That was, indeed, a tall order. I was fighting hard to rein in my thoughts. I had no idea what to do. How does one control the movements of a mind? Why does it always want to think of the one thing you ask it not to remember anymore? I can move my hands and legs in any direction I want; but when it comes to my mind, I'm absolutely powerless. So who's the boss, me or my mind? Why does it always behave like an undisciplined child? Maybe the mind doesn't like being told what to do. Maybe it's simply rebellious by nature. And keeping that mind fixed in one place? Possibly that's out of the question.

But then again, like any other organ, my mind is part of my physical existence. I didn't understand why it wouldn't listen to me at all. At first, I tried to control·it; soon I gave that up and tried to make friends with it. But that didn't help either. Why, I wondered, must Adeline's face pop up with every move I made?

A Skype call from my daughter, Lisa, helped me find a new way to fight that battle. While I was talking with her, I forgot about the rest of the world, and I didn't think of Ade even for a second during that half hour. It became clear to me that a mind cannot process two things at the same time with the same intensity, much like when a nagging back pain takes a backseat as soon as a migraine attack comes on. And that gave me an idea.

I needed to find myself an occupation as intense and as engrossing as my disruptive thoughts of Ade. I decided to concentrate on writing, like I used to do in my childhood days. Writing had always helped me deal with my problems; when I was in school I would carry a notebook around with me so that I could escape to my imaginary world and work through my bottled-up emotions with the help of my make-believe characters. It helped me get perspective.

Then again, I hadn't done much writing in recent years, especially the kind I was fond of. I wrote a couple of articles here and there on financial planning. Both Mimi and I were so focused on our future that any activity not helping in advancing our careers would've never made our to-do list. And spending time on writing? Of course, that would've been unthinkable.

Nonetheless, after breakfast I sat down in front of my laptop. Surprisingly, not even a word came out. Was it the lack of practice or too much chaos in my head? Soon I had a better idea: why sit in a closed room when I could sit under the open sky and embrace nature in all its purity? I packed my laptop, bought a cup of coffee to take along the way, and set off for one of the roadside benches facing the valley on the way to Mürren. What better place on earth for a writer to start a great story?

It was a trekking route, so at times it was a pretty steep climb. But what a profound view! I was stunned. Nature was at free play. I was thoroughly enjoying the view of the tiny town of Lauterbrunnen a thousand feet below and the panorama of an imposing mountain range at a distance. Colorful country cottages were the sole proof of any human existence in the eternal Alps. To my right, huge perpendicular rocks closing in from both sides created a spectacular cleft opening up to far-away glaciers. The Staubbach Falls plunging from a 300-meter high overhanging cliff sprayed water all around, laying a mystic veil on the valley. The isolated trail and the depth of silence made it all so intense. Fortunately, the camera in my head didn't run out of batteries; it kept on clicking.

But soon, mist covered everything, pulling a shade over my eyes. I couldn't even see anything ten feet ahead of me. Then the fog cleared as quickly as it had come, and everything was back to normal. What was that? One minute I could enjoy the nature's finest creation, and the next minute, I could see nothing. I sat there for hours watching the best hide and seek game of all time. No, I didn't start writing yet; but the calmness in the Alps was already soothing my nerves.

As I opened my laptop, Matthew and Lisa's smiling faces on my screen hit me; I had taken that picture last year, in our living room. My morning conversation with Lisa immediately filled my heart. "Why did you leave me, Dad? Come back! I promise I'll be good." I guess, I was still trying to put together arguments in a language easy enough for a five-year-old girl to understand. There was no room for pretension and hypocrisy, and that was the difficulty.

I knew that had it not been for Matthew and Lisa, Mimi and I would've broken up a long time ago; we had simply outgrown each other. It had all started out like any other love story; the first few years after our marriage were like living a fairy tale. Whenever she was home, she would come running to greet me the moment I came back from the office. Then she would shower me with kisses: "Hi! How was your day? I went shopping, you know, but I can't show you now. You have to wait till the lights are off." And then, she would giggle and disappear.

In three quick years it had all flattened to a polite 'Hey!' Our dinner table conversations had dried up; the only thing I could hear was the annoying, ridiculous clink of forks and knives cutting and scraping on our plates. That noise became more and more unbearable, and the screeching sound felt louder and louder. At first, I tried to keep mine under control, but the sound coming from another plate made it even worse. I always had hated that noise—it made me insane—and I thought she was doing it on purpose, just to get on my nerves.

It took me a long time to understand that this wasn't living together; it was coexisting. But unfortunately we weren't ready to break free from each other. Who knows, maybe we were simply not ready to admit our failure.

After a lot of family counseling, we thought, like a million others had, maybe kids could repair the damage that two adults hadn't been able to fix. First came Matthew, followed by Lisa—two wonderful kids—and things did turn around, at least for a while. Innocent joy and laughter filled the house again. Growing kids make a lot of noise; though not all of it is music to our ears, most of it sounds like family fun. Mimi and I both started spending time at home again playing with the kids, having family dinners, and going to movies and picnics.

It is true that kids mend fences and often bridge the gap that adults are so afraid to fill. Most often, it's our adult ego that stops us from doing what should've been done in the first place. Thankfully, kids don't have this problem; their innocent minds are above false self-esteem and self-inflicted inflated ego. In the adult world, we often become cold to one another, but kids can look beyond that invisible wall. Kids don't accept us being cold to them.

Communication is two-way traffic; if one person stops talking, the other automatically shuts down. But if we adults can do what kids do, and restart the conversation, the other person will automatically begin talking as well. Matthew and Lisa helped us rebuild what we had lost, for a little while.

I suddenly noticed a few water droplets on my screen. Low, dark clouds were hanging overhead. I hadn't even noticed the sudden disappearance of sunlight, but up in the mountains the weather is always unpredictable. I knew I had to hurry. There wasn't a shelter in sight; in fact, I hadn't seen anything on my way up.

It started raining before I reached the halfway mark. Even though I quickened my pace, reaching the hotel twenty minutes later, I was completely wet. The moment I entered, the rain stopped. Really? That was so unfair; it had ruined a perfect morning. But I guess life is like that. Every now and then, it throws us a curveball, and expects us to duck or change our game plan quickly, just to test our survival instinct. Well, I survived again. I ordered a cup of coffee and went into my room to change.

A little while later, room service brought me a hot cup of coffee with two cookies on the side. I sat by the window and looked out at the snow-covered mountain peaks. Now that the rain had passed, the afternoon sun had reclaimed its reign on the mountains, dazzling my eyes. I slowly sipped my coffee. It was refreshingly heavenly.

I knew I was lucky to have that stunning view from my room. However, my happiness had a very short life span as my thoughts reappeared like a mist covering my eyes. I could still see the glaciers at a distance, but my optic nerves couldn't get past the thick walls of jumbled-up memories in my brain. What had happened back in Singapore? How had I screwed up everything? What Matthew and Lisa would think of all these?

Had I really neglected them? What could've been more important in our family life than our own kids? Although Mimi and I had been running our individual races, possibly ahead of our peers, what good was our speed if we lost sight of the finish line? We should've given our kids more time; they were such delicate things, especially Lisa. She was only five.

The night before I took off for Europe, Lisa insisted that I go upstairs and tuck her in. Lisa loved bedtime stories. But that night she didn't allow me to read one from her books: "I know all those stories, Dad; tell me a new one." I had no clue how to do that; I was never much of a fairy tale guy. However, I lay down next to her and tried to tell her a story about a young boy who landed in a foreign land where no one understood his language, much like it happened in many fantasy stories. She wrapped her tiny hands around my neck and held me tight, whispering, "Do you have to go tonight, Daddy?"

I knew my heart had been chained forever. "Yes, I do. But hey, I'll come back soon."

"You promise?"

"Yes, baby, I promise."

She closed her eyes and asked me to finish the story, but I didn't know how that young boy's journey would end. He wanted to know the truth about life; yet, he had no idea how or where to find it. Knowing that his life was nothing unless living was meaningful, he struggled to find answers. As time passed, the journey became tiring and even more complicated.

A rapid movement outside Lisa's door suddenly deflected my vision; I thought it might be Mimi, but saw nothing in the shadowy hall. Lisa was fast asleep. Perhaps it was only me, or maybe Mimi was also waiting outside the door, listening to how the story would end. That I would never know.

Mimi had once been a good listener. We used to spend so much time talking—mostly about our own dreams and aspirations, and occasionally, pure nonsense. But as the years passed, I guess, we had so little time to talk and even less time to listen. After the kids were born, we both adjusted our schedules to involve ourselves more with the family. But that didn't change anything between the two of us. We were taking care of our kids like it was another family chore. And that was definitely not fair to them.

Darkness fell in the Alps, and the streetlights went up. The headlights from the distant traffic on the narrow, winding roads played hide and seek in between turns and bends from behind the bushes. I got up from my chair and turned the lights on in my room. There was a heaviness in my head. I pulled on my jacket and walked out of the room to get fresh air.

I felt a little cold at first—there was a nip in the air—but I didn't care. Lauterbrunnen in the evening was very different. Darkness and absolute silence ruled the Alps. I walked around aimlessly on deserted roads for a while until I reached a small cemetery. Crossing it, I found a bench on a narrow street on the other side and sat down. I felt tired for no reason. As much as I wanted to avoid thinking about the mess I was in, my mind wanted to resolve everything once and for all.

But the truth is, not only did I not know how to fix everything, but I also had no idea when and where it all had started. My friends repeatedly told me that compared to what many had, my family life was picture-perfect. Sadly, I hadn't been able to see that picture for a very long time. I often woke up in the middle of the night with a severe headache, staring at the ceiling as if all the answers were encrypted in a language that was far beyond my knowledge. Maybe this was the start of the infamous midlife crisis or a catastrophe in the making; I didn't know. Perhaps I had always thought something was amiss.

I felt I had been heading in the wrong direction in life; though I wondered how that had happened. Had I chosen my destination wrongly or boarded the wrong flight? If it was the latter, it would be easier to rectify, because anybody could understand a silly mistake. But I was worried that I might have chosen the wrong destination. I didn't know what I could do other than head back to the point where and when I marked the destination so wrongly in my journey plan.

Yet, how could I explain any of that to a five-year-old child? It's always the adults who mess up, and kids suffer the consequences. After a day-long deliberation, I had nothing.

Chapter 3

IMMEDIATELY AFTER BREAKFAST the next morning, I decided to take a stroll toward Mürren again. The sudden rain yesterday had forced me to abandon my plan and had interrupted my train of thought. Besides, the ecstatic view from the top was more than worth going back to see.

The road snaked around the mountain base like a python. I had seen so many winding roads from so many hills, but the view never ceased to amaze me; no two patterns were ever the same. And indeed, why wouldn't that be? After all, nature never creates the same thing twice. Look at the big oceans like the Pacific and the Atlantic: the differences in temperature, salinity, and depth are proven facts. And all these scientific facts aside, what about people's perceptions? The moment we talk about a Pacific island holiday, the mind immediately conjures up a picture of balmy days, palm trees, sandy white beaches, and vodka in hand. Can anyone picture that in an Atlantic holiday?

Sitting on the same bench as the day before, I felt silence and peace all around me. But inside, my mind was still quite turbulent; I kept thinking about my failed marriage. Although I wanted to stop all that noise inside my head, I didn't know how. And failing miserably in my pursuit, an hour later, I started to walk back to my hotel.

I had always thought a place like this could help me sort out things more easily, but the problem was that the quieter it became outside, the louder it turned inside. What I was looking for certainly didn't exist in the outside world; it must be an inward scrutiny for better clarity. I had to face myself and answer my questions honestly and diligently.

And to do that I must dig deeper, even if that meant digging through unpleasant memories. Unpleasant it was, not because we broke off; but unfortunately we had separated on bad terms. And that left a bitter aftertaste. I wasn't sure when and how my relationship with Mimi had started going downhill. Both of us clearly knew we were always running two races in life: one was to get ahead, and the other was to stay ahead. Together we watched the movie *Without Limits* at least four or five times. The real-life story captured our hearts; in many ways it spoke to us.

The film was about the great American runner Steve Prefontaine, the former record holder in seven distance track events. His coach, Bill Bowerman, who later founded Nike, always told him to go slowly for the first few laps and hold his energy for the last lap. But Prefontaine refused to listen. He argued it was the front-runner who always received all the love and cheering from the crowd; he wanted to run like that guy, and not like the one who sneaked past him in the last lap.

Mimi and I both knew it wouldn't be easy to stay in front all the time in the race of life. But apparently we did okay. My promotions and hefty bonuses soon made me one of the most talked-about portfolio managers in Singapore, while Mimi took control of her dad's Internet start-up and more than doubled the value of her company shares.

But in our bid to finish as front-runners, we sacrificed our love, until one day we both recognized it was too late to salvage. We had very little time for ourselves; progressively we talked less and less. I was running all right; but I didn't know where to. Worse, Mimi and I both made the same mistake. We ran our individual races; we ran fast, but we always ran in parallel lines. Alas! Why didn't we ever realize that two parallel lines would never meet? It left us disengaged from each other. Like we all sync our watches every year, at the start and at the end of daylight saving time, we also need to sync our relationships once in a while. And Mimi and I definitely hadn't been in sync for a long time.

Slowly we had drifted apart and started making our own plans for the evenings; less time together seemed like a better idea. I went out with my buddies and colleagues, and she spent time with hers. However, all hell broke loose on her friend Laura's birthday. That evening when I came home, she shouted from the bedroom, "What took you so long? Hurry up—we're already late."

"Late for what?"

"Laura's birthday party. It's on your calendar."

But I wasn't feeling well that evening; I thought I was coming down with a fever or something, and a little rest might make everything go away. Besides, I had another important meeting the next morning. However, I wasn't in the mood to explain all that to her. "Sorry, I can't go; I'm not feeling up to it."

Obviously, the shorter version didn't go down so well with her. Mimi was furious; she screamed from the bedroom, "Go to hell! If you wanted to embarrass me, the joke is on you, mister; I can always find a date anytime I want. Don't wait up."

However, realizing my mistake, I got out of my chair in the study and walked toward the bedroom to explain myself. But at the loud thud of the main door, I gathered there was nothing much I could do to save the evening. I took too long.

Now, thinking about that incident in Lauterbrunnen gave me a chill again. Is marriage meant to be like this, or do all relationships come with an expiration date? Unknowingly, I stopped in the middle of the road. With the thought of that lousy evening in my mind, I couldn't walk any farther. I felt the same excruciating pain all over again throughout my body and mind. I had always regretted that fight. If we had been a little more tolerant, we could've easily avoided it. And soon, my heartache turned into an acute headache; my legs suddenly felt too heavy to move. Thank god I was carrying a bottle of water. I took a sip and felt better. My mouth had been all dried out.

I wanted to sit down; but I couldn't see another bench on that trekking route. Finally, I noticed a big firewood stockpile by the roadside and decided to take out a few pieces and rest awhile.

However, opposite the stockpile there was a small iron gate; it looked new with a fresh coat of paint, and next to it was a small concrete slab, no doubt a leftover from the previous gate. It served my purpose well, and of course, it was much better than a bunch of uneven logs. I immediately sat down and took another sip from my water bottle.

It was, indeed, true that with each passing day, Mimi and I were thrown further apart. Sitting there as I replayed the past few years in my head, I was still as clueless as I was before; I had no idea why we had turned on each other like enemies, even for the simplest of things. When I forgot to get milk one day on my way back from the office, she suddenly became furious. "Can you not do even one thing for the house? I left you a voice message, and I texted you as well."

"I'm sorry, babe; it slipped my mind. Don't worry, I'll get it now."

"Don't bother. You better go back where your mind is."

I knew what she was hinting at; she thought I had been out with my colleagues again. But those past few days we had been terribly busy pitching a new client. I kept quiet, unable to understand what had changed in our relationship or what had gone wrong. Love, friendship, and understanding: all that was so close to our heart a few years before suddenly felt like out of our reach. I apologized one more time and headed for the bedroom.

The last few years had been terrible. I was no longer living; I was simply killing time, hoping and praying all the bickering would be over soon like a bad dream. I didn't have the faintest idea how I had gotten there; all I had wanted after my mediocre school days was to feel and live like a front-runner, winning at the end of every lap in every game. Was that really asking too much? Those days I couldn't think of living without

Mimi; but living with her in that condition was like living with a continuous chest pain waiting for more drama to unfold.

When we had first met, the dreams I dreamed with her were neither lies nor deceptions, just uncharted territory for me. We also had a great time together. I could never forget my magical first date with her. Indeed, that was my best date ever. My life suddenly became more exciting. Our romantic picnic also ended up in a spine-chilling thriller. Although I enjoyed every bit of it in the beginning, slowly time laid dust on everything, and the daily grind took the shine away and uncovered the bitter truth of life.

I also learned that marriage was a huge balancing act. We both carefully chose what to say and what not to say to each other. If I worked late at the office, I left out certain names— names that could raise suspicion that it was more play than work, especially if Tina was involved.

Tina and I had worked side by side for more than three years, and occasionally until late at night. Actually, Tina was my recruit; I had selected her—fresh out of college— from a shortlist of three other candidates. She had been a brilliant student and she always took her work seriously. But that didn't stop her from being a girl. She was so young, barely twenty-two. Her playful crush on me wasn't really much of a secret in our office; but that was all it was. To me, she was like any other colleague. I introduced her to Mimi at an office party within the first few days. They liked each other and became Facebook friends.

But a couple of years later, one day Mimi noticed a shocking posting on Tina's Facebook page: "I've a plus-one invitation this weekend to my friend's wedding. And guess what? No dates. I know whom I would've loved to bring, though. I've a huge crush on him. He's so good-looking and looks so Ben Affleck in real life. I think he's about six-two. And oh, those piercing eyes! But sigh! That ain't going to work. And get this, he is happily married. I can't be a homewrecker, right? Besides, he works in the same office. Forget it, guys; I'll be flying solo."

Mimi told me, "You know what, it doesn't take a genius to figure out whom she is talking about. You're too lenient. If anyone made such a comment in my office, I would sack them right away."

Perhaps Mimi was right. But I didn't have the heart to fire Tina on a sex harassment issue; I knew what that would do to her career in the corporate world. I sincerely believed she had no evil intention. She had possibly forgotten all about Mimi by then.

The young generation is like that; they've tons of friends they don't care about. It's a numbers game to them. And they've this constant craving to tell everyone everything about themselves: where they're eating, what the food looks like, whom they're dating, and all about their feelings. I guess it's a way of getting the satisfaction of being followed like celebrities. The difference is that instead of being chased by paparazzi cameras, they've to take selfies and post them on their own. I thought Tina's actions were just silly, but not in any way wicked or spiteful.

But unfortunately Mimi didn't see it that way; Tina was attractive, younger, and we spent more than twelve hours a day together. Mimi said, "People talk." I had no idea, though, who those people were and what they were talking about. I was sure Mimi didn't look at Tina's Facebook page again; otherwise she would've known that two months later, Tina got married to a guy she had known in her school days.

When I had first heard that, I felt relieved, but more than anything, I had a sense of victory; I thought that I had proven Mimi wrong. But today, sitting there in the Alps, I laughed at my stupidity. As if that was the sole reason we broke up!

Possibly initially as revenge, Mimi started coming home late, and sometimes, very late. The qualities we used to admire in each other soon became unbearable. Mimi had always loved my carefree attitude toward life; but after couple of years together, she began equating that with irresponsibility. I used to love Mimi's sense of style and fashion, but as time passed, I looked at that as an obsession. I guess we were deliberately trying to hurt each other.

In retrospect, I could've handled the situation better; I could've reassured Mimi of our own relationship. The problem was that it had already developed cracks. And I didn't do anything to repair those rifts. On the contrary, I did everything I could to alienate her; I also said many hurtful things.

I heard a sudden noise, and a small truck loaded with chopped firewood suddenly pulled up in front of the stockpile near me. I was in no mood for company, so I grabbed my backpack and started walking down again toward my hotel. It was close to lunchtime, anyway.

I still didn't understand one thing: why, when two people start living together, do they end up hurting each other so much? Maybe that's an indication that too much of anything isn't good, like too much food or too much wine—all of which can be potentially dangerous for the human body. Likewise, maybe the 24-7 association with our loved ones is most likely fatal for any long-term relationship. Otherwise, why would two people who love and care for each other sabotage their relationship?

Or is the problem even more deeply rooted? Maybe in modern society we love ourselves so much that we don't really care about the next person; we've learned to insulate ourselves and leave the rest of the world alone. When we ask a friend or a colleague, 'How are you doing?' do we honestly want to know all about their illnesses or feelings? When we ask, 'How was your weekend?' do we truly want the details? Certainly not; it's just polite conversation, a superficial icebreaker that has been so ingrained in us that we've forgotten how to stay honest with each other.

Instead of talking it out, Mimi and I had both chosen to keep quiet. The fact is, when the wind blows against us, everything seems ten times more difficult, and everything goes against our wishes. The nights I came home early from work, Mimi turned up late; and possibly the evenings Mimi thought she would make an effort to catch up and talk, I returned in the wee hours of the morning. Sometimes before going to sleep, I softly said, "Good night;" in fact, so softly that I knew for sure that it wouldn't reach Mimi's ears. Who knows, maybe Mimi did the same. I often thought of putting my arms around her and kissing her as hard as I always used to do. I would wonder, couldn't we shake ourselves like a can of soda and then pull the tab, letting everything bottled up inside come out like a fizz? Then I would suddenly stop, thinking what would happen if Mimi didn't kiss me back. . . and I would freeze.

I was so preoccupied with my thoughts that I didn't even notice I had walked past my hotel until I had nearly reached the Staubbach Falls and the gigantic rock faces. There's something in the air in Lauterbrunnen that helps relax the brain and brings out the intricate innermost thoughts out in the open. The gigantic stone walls on one side, the vast green pastures on the other, and the melting glaciers in front made me realize how insignificant my life had become in terms of eternity.

Throughout my adult life, I had always felt like a winner. However, for the past couple of years, I had been struggling to hold on to that thought; I started to feel very small. The sheer magnitude of the natural beauty in front of my eyes reinforced that. What was my role in this eternal odyssey? I suddenly saw hundreds and thousands of Rohans who had done their MBAs, married their sweethearts, and had beautiful kids—and they seemed perfectly happy. Was I wrong all along in believing that I was a winner? Maybe, or maybe not; I wasn't so sure anymore.

The fact is, the world doesn't care about our winning or losing, and neither does it work for us or against us. It's all in our head. The truth remains: I am one of over seven billion people on earth. How am I any different from the rest?

Although the digital world wanted me to believe the universe revolved round me by putting me at the center every time I opened Google Maps, as I stood there in front of the majestic Alps, I couldn't subscribe to that notion anymore. I was sure the profound beauty of Lauterbrunnen would still make hundreds and thousands of people happy every day, with or without me standing there at the center point. So, what did that make me—just another person?

Maybe I was smart; but there're millions of smart people, and there're millions of smarter people, and thousand others whom we could call super-smart. Their individual achievements could make me look really insignificant any day. Then what's the purpose of my being here?

What would make me matter in the universe? What would make my existence meaningful? I knew deep in my heart that living was never about money. I often had thought that we attach more value to money than it actually deserves. Many say money is like oxygen. I could never agree. Without oxygen one would die within few minutes; but anyone can live without money for days.

But Mimi always said, "Money is power. Give someone a hundred-dollar bill who deserves fifty, and they'll treat you like god in a suit."

Who knows, maybe money is like magic; it creates illusions, like I once experienced with Mimi at a David Blaine show. Blaine pulled an iguana from a lady's purse; then he set fire to a twenty-dollar bill and made it all fine the next minute. Maybe money makes us believe that we can do anything and everything; and the more money we have, the more power we possess. Does it really work like that, or is that an illusion too?

When you work hard and buy a nice car for yourself, people often think money bought you that car. But this thinking could be wrong. It was your hard work that bought you the car, not the money. So what makes us believe in illusion, and what makes truth so elusive, as if we are all under a magic spell? I couldn't separate the two anymore. No wonder I was still feeling lost.

As I finally walked into the hotel, I was greeted by the owner himself, Mr. Johnson. "Good afternoon, sir. How are you today?"

Mr. Johnson was a self-made man and had been running the small resort for the past twenty-two years. About eight years before, he had opened a second one at Mürren, which was busier during the winter season; but overall the Lauterbrunnen resort was still the money maker for him because it had the summer crowd as well. He was friendly and very easy to talk to. Maybe that was a prerequisite in his line of business.

After short pleasantries, I headed for the dining hall. I was feeling quite hungry. The waiter showed me to a window-side table. But as I sat down, and looked out of the window, I noticed a number of hang gliders in the area. They all looked so graceful up there, like majestic birds flying with the flow of the wind. The bright and colorful wings against the sunny summer-green backdrop of the Alps made me think that I could also get a bird's-eye view of the whole place. Not a bad idea, indeed. I knew I had to do something to get my mind off those depressing thoughts. Maybe that's what I had needed for a long time: a new perspective.

I immediately ran back to Mr. Johnson and asked him whether he knew anyone who could help me learn hang gliding.

Mr. Johnson said, "That would be Kevin's job. He is a great kid. Go get his contact number from the front desk."

As soon as I had that settled, I headed back to my table. But first, I ordered a bottle of Chardonnay and asked the waiter to serve two glasses. I sent one to Mr. Johnson for all his help since I had arrived; and he raised his glass from a distance.

Chapter 4

AS THE MORNING SUNLIGHT came through my window, I woke up strangely charged and excited. The peaks at a distance were still covered in snow, but the bright sunlight had washed the rest of the mountain and the valley green. I envisioned a great new day. I had been stuck in an illusion far too long; my vision had been blurred by my own weaknesses. The idea of hang gliding had truly sprung me back to life. I couldn't wait any longer.

Once I saw an advertisement on a billboard in New York, and the headline stuck with me: 'When was the last time you did something for the first time?' I hadn't had that experience in a long time, like when I first kissed Mimi, or when I held Matthew and Lisa in my arms for the first time. I still get goose bumps thinking about those moments.

Now I was hoping to have that feeling one more time. I was new to hang gliding. Maybe there were some risks involved. So what? Living is a risky business; yet we do it every day without even thinking about it.

The girl at the reception desk had told me that it was actually tandem hang gliding, or paragliding. I would be accompanied by a professional paraglider; they wouldn't let me jump from a thousand-foot cliff in the Alps all by myself.

Honestly, I wasn't much worried. In fact, I felt alive; the feeling was of anticipation, excitement, and thrill, I hadn't encountered in a long time.

The sail looked much bigger up close, and absolutely overwhelming. Once we reached the top of the mountain, my guide, Kevin, checked the wind pressure and looked satisfied. I did exactly as Kevin told me to do. First, we walked a few paces and then ran a few more steps downhill until we felt the chute gathered enough wind to lift us off the ground.

Moments later, we were in the air flying like birds over the cliffs and looking down at the valley from a thousand feet above. The feeling was incredible; I could see the green Alpine meadows, the waterfalls, and the valleys, in miniature and yet so real, like playing Monopoly on PlayStation. Looking through the glass windows of an airplane is one thing, and experiencing the wind pressure out in the open, sailing through it like an eagle, and seeing things from a 180-degree angle is quite another.

In fact, I got a glimpse of another thing important that day: a clear view of my life in perfect 3-D. Our biased sentiments and ego often cover parts of our lives in shadows and darkness. Ignorance often hides the truth, which refuses to come out in the open. But once I got to see my life from the top, the unobstructed view brought a whole new dimension. Suddenly everything started to make sense.

When I had started dating Mimi, I became extremely happy at the unexpected turn in my life; but at the same time, I was fearful that she would soon slip away. She belonged to a different class; and she had expensive habits and a different lifestyle than I was used to. Although I coveted her company every minute, I also dreaded meeting her every evening. I knew Mimi could be a little extravagant at times, and I was prepared to accept her for who she was, but right at that point in time everything seemed freakishly expensive for me. There was still close to a month left before I could start work, and about two months before I would see any paycheck. Although she volunteered to pay most of the time, that didn't go down well with my male ego; and I always promised her, "Don't worry; soon I'll earn a lot of money."

"I'm not worried; I've money."

But I wanted to assure her. "I want to give you everything in life."

"Don't worry, Rohan; I've everything in life."

Still, I decided to make good on that promise for the rest of my life. I don't know why; but I wanted her to acknowledge that I could do more than her family had ever done for her. She never asked me to move from my stock analyst job to portfolio management. I did that to myself to earn more money, and soon, in my head, I was competing against everyone else. Now when I looked at my life from a distance, I realized that wasn't an ambition; it was a messed-up ego trip.

Suddenly a stark contrast appeared before my eyes. I looked at Kevin; he was like the free bird I used to be a long time ago. Time and marriage had clipped my wings; they had pulled a veil in front of my eyes. Does this happen to everyone? I asked Kevin what his secret was. Kevin was in his early twenties, and lived in Mürren—a ski teacher in the winter and a paragliding pilot in the summer. He was all about the thrills. He said, "Life is about living, not about sitting on the sidelines."

To Kevin, there was nothing more exciting than cheating death. He said, "Like it or not, we're all participants in the world's most thrilling game."

"What's that?" I asked naively.

"Life itself," he answered with a smile. "It's the most thrilling, because no bookie will dare take a bet on your life."

Indeed, no one knew that better than him. His parents, professional skiers, had both died in an avalanche in Canada when he was a young boy; but that didn't stop him from skiing. If anything, the accident inspired him even more. He said, "If we don't come face-to-face with death once in a while, we tend to forget the gifts of life. We get so used to our mundane daily routine that we ignore the finer parts of the mind and soul. We slowly begin to take everything for granted: the food we eat, the family we live with, the nature that fascinates us. And we waste all our time and energy on ego trips and senseless squabbles. But the moment we come close to death, we forget all trivialities; we forgive everyone, we love every creature on earth, and we let go our pride and embrace harmony. When we cheat death, we learn to appreciate our food again, and we feel glad that we have a family to go to."

Kevin was an adventure sport freak. Hang gliding, skiing, snowboarding, and skydiving: he loved them all. He would jump off a cliff to see if he could remain alive. Many would say he had a death wish; but Kevin always said, "Every now and then I'm just putting a little life back in my life." Come to think of it, Kevin and I had nothing in common; but I admired him. His daredevil attitude drew me in.

With my newfound clarity, the days in Lauterbrunnen became much lighter for me. I stopped brooding for a while and looked for a peaceful solution. I had never imagined that I would find myself asking the most difficult life questions in the world's most beautiful place. I had no idea that I could find friendship here, even without looking. Life here had a rhythm that had no sound; living wasn't a chore, it was a celebration. It was about movements without moving; it was about the peaceful halt in between the running. It was about finding peace without having to search for it.

No doubt I found peace in Lauterbrunnen, but whenever I saw a couple holding hands, that invariably reminded me of Adeline. Once, while walking through a busy street in Vienna, I'd had to let go of her hand to cross a dug-up manhole. Seconds later, when she caught up and held my hand again, she said, "I wouldn't have let you go."

I tried to explain. "Didn't you see the fencing? I would've fallen there."

"So? I wouldn't mind falling for you."

That day I had kept quiet; I knew what she had wanted to say. Indeed, by holding hands a couple can always say a lot of things they couldn't have otherwise said in a public place. Among a million people, they can touch and tickle each other at their most intimate places: their hearts.

Now I missed that touch; I missed her. I still had glimpses of Adeline's innocent face looking into my eyes for answers; the sound of her laughter haunted me even six hundred miles away. Her Gmail and Skype icons popped up green whenever I went online; but I wasn't ready to face her yet. I didn't just want to shut out Adeline; I wanted to shut myself out too, at least for a few more days.

I needed to quickly resolve all this and move forward; I had a long road ahead. I made my virtual presence invisible for the very first time in my life. I told my kids to call my cell phone. I thought if I kept all doors and windows closed, nobody would ever bother me.

But nothing else bothers us more than our own mind. I couldn't stop asking myself the same question over and again: why was it that I didn't want to face Adeline? The truth is that I hadn't had Adeline's name anywhere in my journey plan; the halt took me by surprise as well. I was recovering from a bad marriage; I was in no way ready for another relationship. That's why, when Adeline declared her sincere love for me without any hesitation, I kept quiet. I didn't know what else I could've done.

I never took Ade as another happy-go-lucky party girl; she was also intelligent and supersensitive, usually a lethal combination. These people are often very delicate and can get hurt easily. Their minds are pure; what they see or experience of others is often a reflection of their own minds. They think everything is beautiful. Their minds don't allow them to see the ugliness in the world; they trust everybody; they love each creature in the universe. The underlying truth behind this is universal: a human mind in general is pure, and a pure mind is attracted to anything beautiful. A good-looking face, a beautiful flower, or a stunning scenery—all have the same appeal. Naturally, I thought, if all that she could see was the reflection of her own mind, how would she ever understand my complicated world?

Besides, maybe I was too scared to commit to another relationship. Or could that be the lingering thoughts of Mimi? Certainly not; although I was still very fond of Mimi, and she'll always remain the mother of my kids, I was definitely not in love with her anymore. That chapter had closed once and for all.

But whose fault was that? Now that I had new perspectives, I was willing to take my share of the blame. The human mind often acts like a volcano. Sometimes it erupts and disintegrates everything that comes near it. But one particular thought can also stay latent for ages and become active all over again at a much later date. Something similar had happened to me; after about three years of marriage, my childhood thoughts had started haunting me again. But I never told Mimi about any of that; I decided to deal with it on my own. Besides, I wasn't sure where I stood on my faith at that point in time.

Finding me absent-minded, Mimi often asked, "What's wrong, hon? Is everything okay?"

I would immediately pull myself out of that darkness and say, "Of course; everything is fine," and I thought everything was under control. Consequently, instead of blowing up, those thoughts crawled back inside and started eating me alive. Slowly I lost myself, and I wasn't sure what I was doing—barely surviving on life support or racing ahead triumphantly like Steve Prefontaine?

But if life is about reaching from point A to point B, how many of us really know where life's point B is? Possibly very few. More often than not, we're actually traveling from point A to the unknown. If you ask yourself every day where you want to go, you might come up with a new answer every time. That's why I was convinced that there could be no happily ever after in life. We live in an ever-changing world. Everything in life is dynamic. One minute isn't just sixty seconds. A lot can happen in one minute; a life can change forever. In one minute, a drunk driver can rip through a stationary car at a red light and put the other driver in a lifelong coma. In one minute, one's eyes can meet someone else's at the end of a bar counter, leading to a lifelong commitment. In one minute, a flying bullet can miss its original target and tear an innocent bystander apart instead.

And that's only the outside world. Within our body, the liver filters 1.4 liters of blood, the body produces more than two billion blood cells, and each blood cell makes a complete circuit of the body, all within one minute. In one minute, the mind can go visit ten places around the world. Then, is it at all possible for love to stay the same, with the same depth and intensity? If not, then why do we keep hanging on to that fairy-tale ending? Who says marriages are forever?

Maybe no one. Maybe it's just another wishful thinking. My time with Kevin made me realize one thing: life is, indeed, short, and nothing is permanent. We must experiment and experience life as it comes. Every day is a new day; and yet none of us are sure whether we'll live to see the next one. We must take chances, and like Kevin said, once in a while, put a little life back in our lives. We cannot simply sit on the sidelines, waiting for a miracle to happen and watching life pass us by.

However, we don't have much control over many aspects of our lives, let alone love and whom we love. Then why couldn't I be with Adeline? Maybe it wasn't the right time. Then again, falling in love doesn't work according to a schedule, like board meetings. I wished I had thought about this back in Vienna. The moment I felt that I was falling for her, I ran at the first chance I got. The arguments in my head were all so stupid and silly. She would never have bought the age difference thing, and I knew that too. But I still couldn't figure out what was holding me back. If I was given a second chance to live again, why didn't I take it? Was I scared to fail again, or was it the many unresolved issues I needed to sort out first? After a lot of thinking, I was leaning toward the latter.

Chapter 5

TWO DAYS LATER, I decided to have breakfast in a small restaurant along the main road, but farther away from the railway station and the town center with its variety stores, bakeries, cafes, and restaurants all lined up. This was a quaint and quiet cafe with only few tables; good thing, it wasn't crowded. I was particularly drawn by its huge glass windows overlooking the mountains. I stepped in and I realized I was the first customer that morning.

I sat close to the window facing the valley. The view in Lauterbrunnen from any point was truly amazing. Every now and then, I could see a cog railway train chugging along, tearing the green mountain terrain from Lauterbrunnen to the top of Jungfrau. I ordered my breakfast and flipped through the only English newspaper in the restaurant. I was enjoying my morning coffee in absolute silence and solitude until two gentlemen walked in.

I heard them talking, though I couldn't quite see their faces. From their conversation, I figured they were brothers. One, who had a strong British accent, had been laid off from the factory he had worked at for the past ten years. He was also going through a nasty breakup and a custody battle over his son. His brother, who sounded older than him, was trying to console him. I didn't mean to eavesdrop on their conversation, but the pin-drop silence in the restaurant didn't leave me with any other option. Besides, the elder brother's words pulled me in.

He said, "Listen, life is like two sides of a coin; you get both heads and tails. Let's assume heads is for happiness and tails is for trouble. Maybe you'll get happiness in the next flip. Trust me; no one ever gets heads or tails all the time. You should be happy knowing that happiness is waiting for you."

The younger brother laughed and interrupted him. "But I'd so many consecutive tails that I almost lost count, brother."

The elderly gentleman said, "I understand that. But have patience; it's going to get better soon. If you look around, you'll notice that nothing is permanent in this universe. You see the clouds and the drizzle outside? That won't be here for long. I bet you'll see the sun again."

The younger brother seemed impatient; he jumped up from his chair and started walking up and down the length of the restaurant. He was mumbling something, but I couldn't hear him. Finally, he came back and sat down again.

The older brother continued, "When you see nature up close you understand that nothing is forever, be it a good time or a bad time; nothing stays the same. Leaves change, seasons change, and so do people. And when people change, our relationships change with that."

Immediately, I remembered how Mimi and I had tried to cling to our old relationship. We had steered the best we could; we had turned every corner carefully, negotiated every bend cautiously. But we still hadn't been able to control the outcome. I guess we ignored the fact that we both had changed over time.

Two faces came to my mind: Mr. Barco, my old school teacher in Goa, and my father. They always had the perfect explanation for everything, in sadness and in happiness. The elder brother here did the same thing; he took his brother's heartache and connected that with his immediate surroundings. It didn't look like his brother's personal burden anymore; it became part of a universal process. To my father and Mr. Barco, nothing was random; everything was about cause and effect. I could never figure out how they could see what we all missed. Maybe it was because they were never swayed too much by good news or bad news; they had the unique ability to distance themselves from life. It was as though they had two personalities: one lived within their body, in this world, and the other lived outside, watching everything from a distance.

The truth is, whenever we see someone's house on fire, and their loved ones trapped inside, our heart goes out to that person; but when our own house is burning, we can't stay as calm. We lose all our senses to our emotions. The moment anything bad happened to my father and Mr. Barco, these wise men always tried to put themselves outside their house just as anyone watching from a distance. Of course, I had no way to verify whether that actually hurt them any less. But I would've loved to try that.

I finished my breakfast and ordered another cup of coffee to take with me. The elderly gentleman was right; the sun was out again. A gust of wind brought in the wet smell of the land and the road. I buttoned my jacket and looked out the window; there wasn't a shred of cloud anywhere in the sky. I decided to get out in the open and clear my head.

But as I got up from my chair and started walking toward the cashier, I froze. Earlier I couldn't get a good look at the men sitting behind me, but the moment I glanced at the elderly gentleman facing me, I thought I was hallucinating. My head started spinning. I wanted to sit down again.

The elderly gentleman stood up as well. He was looking directly at me. "Excuse me," he said in a polite tone. "You look so much like one of my old students. They all must've grown up like you, young man. Are you. . ." Then he paused, and since I was too dazed to make any connection or respond, but simply stood there with a blank look, he withdrew himself. "I apologize; I think I made a mistake."

I managed to utter two words: "Mr. Barco?" With his gray hair and without the ubiquitous beard, I almost couldn't recognize him. I had never seen him clean-shaven like this.

"Yes, Rohan, I'm Mr. Barco," said the old man, and he opened his arms. He hugged me and said, "I know I'm old and forgetful, and my eyesight isn't that great either, but I couldn't have mistaken you."

My lips quivered. "You...here?" I still couldn't believe my eyes.

Mr. Barco answered, "Now we live here, Rohan."

Joseph Barco was of Portuguese descent. His father had come to India in his early twenties and fallen in love with a beautiful Goan girl. When his father had left India after his mother passed away, Joseph Barco didn't go back with him; he embraced Indian culture and heritage and took a permanent position in a local school as a chemistry teacher, where he allowed his students to ask all sorts of questions. He used to say, "The more questions you have, the more answers you'll get in life." That was his way of teaching subjects that were not covered in our syllabus. Our little heads didn't quite get it then.

Joseph Barco had continued to live in India until one day he met his wife, Tess, who came from Zurich to visit Goa and whisked him away in 1992. Now they made Switzerland their home and had settled in Lauterbrunnen. Mr. Barco told me that he and his wife lived quite close by, hardly a ten-minute walk from where we were sitting. He had been teaching in a secondary school in Interlaken; his wife managed the restaurant where we were eating.

I also gave him a brief account of what had happened in my life since my parents had migrated to Singapore with me and my sister, Rita; I was seventeen then. Mr. Barco seemed really saddened by the news of my father's death; I'd had no idea they were that close. But all he said was, "He was a fine man, a rare breed in this world."

I was so happy to see him again that I could hardly think of anything else. I was supposed to leave Lauterbrunnen the next day, but all that had changed instantly once I saw Mr. Barco. Now I wanted to stay as long as I could. After all, I had nowhere to rush to.

The person he had been talking to all morning was his half-brother, Ivan, who lived in London and looked much younger. Mr. Barco had invited his brother to stay with them for few days to help him forget his bitter divorce and start afresh. I immediately thought of my new friend, Kevin. Could he be of help here? I told Mr. Barco and his brother about Kevin's philosophy of putting a little life back into living, and suggested that Ivan could go paragliding.

"Oh my god, that's a jolly good idea. Indeed, I saw a couple of guys landing yesterday next to our house. Where do we get this fellow?" Ivan immediately jumped up from his seat.

Mr. Barco smiled; probably he had not seen his brother this happy in a long time. I immediately called Kevin and arranged everything for the next day.

Mr. Barco wasn't interested in paragliding; he said, "I'm too old for that. I would rather spend time with Rohan."

Seeing Mr. Barco that day in Lauterbrunnen opened the floodgates of my childhood memories. That night, as my head touched the pillow and my eyes closed, the darkness of the room took me to a place I had known a long time ago. High school was never easy for me. I went to a very average, small-town, public school, where students were crowded together like buyers in a flea market, and teachers were always tired and overworked, with the exception of maybe one or two of them.

One of those exceptions was Joseph Barco. Looking back, I understood now why he abandoned the crowded teachers' room and isolated himself in a small storage room with apparently no luxury other than his electric kettle, which he often used, to boil water for his herbal tea. Unlike the rest of the students, I always felt a connection with him. I spent hours in that small, dingy room, not studying, but listening to his interpretation of life. I knew that Joseph Barco was no ordinary chemistry teacher; he was a deep thinker who had great admiration for the ancient cultures of China and India and was an ardent devotee of Greek and German philosophers.

One particular afternoon stood out in my memory, the day Mr. Barco began, "Do you know, Rohan, that the most important things in life are free?"

I almost laughed that day. "How is that remotely possible, sir?" I tried to put up an argument instead of dismissing it outright, though deep in my heart, I knew that when Mr. Barco said anything it had to mean something and couldn't be simply tossed away.

Instead of answering, Mr. Barco rose from his chair and walked past me. As I turned my head to see where he was going, I suddenly sensed that he was standing behind my back, and was very close, indeed. His face was near mine. I cringed in fear. I didn't know what to do.

Suddenly he covered my mouth with one hand and my nose with the other. I know now that he didn't want to hurt me, but at the time, I panicked. I started to throw my hands and legs in the air to grasp anything. What had I done wrong? It was just an argument. We had debated many topics before, but he had never reacted this way. Was he upset at my comment, and trying to punish me? His hands held me so tightly to the back of my chair that I couldn't move my head at all, let alone scream for help. For a moment I regretted my comments and was willing to withdraw unconditionally, provided I lived.

Seconds later, Mr. Barco let me go, and I breathed again. He slowly walked back to his seat, and sat down without a word.

I was furious. "Jeez, what did you do that for?"

"To show you what you really needed," Mr. Barco replied calmly.

"And that would be?" I was still recovering from the shock.

Mr. Barco leaned back against his chair and displayed his usual smile. "Well, when you were gasping for air you were desperately looking for oxygen; and the moment I released you to breathe again, you took a lungful, and you felt fine, didn't you?"

I nodded, and Mr. Barco continued. "Now let me ask you one question: how much did you pay for the oxygen that helped you back to life?"

I had not seen that coming. I quietly sat there listening. If he could prove himself right, the world I knew so far would turn upside down.

Mr. Barco continued, "Similarly, the seeds for cultivation are free, the rainwater is free, and the sunlight is free; to think of it, all the essentials in life are free. If you want to know more, go study. Even the books in a library are free," and he smiled.

I had spent the next few days thinking about what Mr. Barco had said. Was it really true? It seemed unbelievable that day, yet it all made sense later in my life.

Looking back now, the question I still had was what my role in the universe should be. I wanted to know how each one of us is connected to the universe that makes the sun and the moon rise every day and lights up our skies with a zillion stars every night. Maybe Mr. Barco would have the answer.

Chapter 6

At Tess's request, Mr. Barco and I met again at her café the next morning. She served us a great breakfast and left the two of us pretty much alone, as she also had other customers to attend to. But I didn't feel like eating anything; my mind was preoccupied with hundreds of questions. Truly, I had been waiting for this meeting the whole night, but sitting face-to-face, I couldn't even say a word. I simply didn't know where to begin. We both knew the breakfast was an excuse; all we wanted was to catch up.

What I had told Mr. Barco the day before was barely the tip of the iceberg; there were a lot of other things left unsaid. And we both knew those were also as important to put the pieces together.

Life brings us to a crossroads every once in a while. Each decision we make, right or wrong, teaches us new lessons, but there comes a point when making any decision becomes tricky. Decisions may be made based on our past mistakes; that one is easy. But when that decision must also take into account how it's going to affect the people we love and care about, it's much harder.

I had never been so confused in my whole life. A few years before, I had thought everything in life was going my way; I was cruising fast, and the world outside the window looked great. Then one day, I woke up and found out that I had been driving all along in the wrong lane. My marriage had been a disaster. Maybe I also had chosen my career wrongly. I soon found out that truth and honesty were grossly overrated when it came to managing other people's money. Who wants a career that depends on lies and deceptions?

But those thoughts alone couldn't help me now; I needed a way out. Should I take up a new career at thirty-six? How should I deal with the absence of Matthew and Lisa in my life? I was most certainly answerable for hurting the three people dearest to me. And I owed an explanation to Adeline, too, for leaving Vienna so abruptly. I had a feeling that I was doing it all wrong; I couldn't alienate everybody. I must find a way out of this maze quickly.

I looked at my watch; my time with Mr. Barco was also running out fast: His brother would be back in few hours. It was like my school exam days all over again: too many questions and too little time, and the tick-tock, tick-tock was getting louder in my head. I wanted to kick myself for not meeting him sooner, yet I couldn't even get started. Although we had talked about many things before, we had never discussed our personal lives. I didn't know how he would respond. I had heard him talking about his brother's personal problems before; that gave me some confidence. I wanted to ask him so many questions; but I was a little hesitant to bring my personal life out in the open.

He sat there quietly all this time, observing me, and then, he suddenly asked, "What brings you to Lauterbrunnen, Rohan?"

"Honestly, I'm not very sure, sir," I said, and everything began to spill out. "I guess I wanted to run away from everything: my job, my life, the divorce, and more recently, even from Adeline. It all seems so futile and pointless after a while."

"Whoa, whoa, slow down, Rohan. What's that? You're talking like you've given up on life." He took out his glasses with one hand and pushed aside his coffee mug with the other, and said, "You can lose everything in life, Rohan; but you can't lose one thing: hope. The moment you lose hope, you lose focus."

"Hope for what, sir?" I asked. "I always thought I knew where I was going; but now the roads look all mixed up."

"You are not alone there, my son. Most of us don't know what we want from life. That's one reason why life seems so challenging. If you know the way to your destination, it's easy to find. Did you ever go looking for a house without having its full address? It wasn't hard because that house didn't exist; it was tough because you had no knowledge of where the house was. You also have to remember that not everyone wants the same thing out of life; some seek money and fame, others, knowledge or family. What do you want? Once you know what you are looking for, it becomes much easier to look."

The answer to that question I thought I knew once. But it wasn't so clear anymore. Of course, like everybody else, I also wanted a good job and a happy family life; but above all, I wanted to know what all this meant; where in the whole universe my life figured. For that matter, everyone else's as well. I couldn't believe a person could live and die, and that would make no difference to the universe. I was overwhelmed with my hundreds of questions, both personal and some not-so-personal. In my limited time with Mr. Barco, I certainly couldn't find answers to all of them. But I knew there was always one thing that could bring clarity to all.

I asked, "Suppose I seek knowledge?"

"You must be more specific, Rohan, because if you say you're looking for a person living in a red house, but without an address, it may take you years to find that particular red house. What sort of knowledge are you seeking? Decide, and narrow your search area by elimination; and then start your journey accordingly.

"Answers to our questions are always here in front of our eyes. We often don't see them because we aren't asking the right questions, or we aren't asking with the intensity it requires. Say, for example, plants and trees have always been living things and have given us fruits and seeds for millions of years; yet we needed a scientist like A. J. C. Bose to prove this to us with a crescograph. Similarly, gravity has always been a force of nature; we just didn't know about its existence until Sir Isaac Newton explained it."

Indeed, he had a point. Mr. Barco always made things simple. But it was definitely not simple enough to help me figure out what I had been missing in my puzzle. So, what did that make me? Blind or blindfolded? Could be the latter, but I didn't care; I wanted to know my answer. Had he forgotten that I was an average guy, not a genius like Isaac Newton or A. J. C. Bose? I didn't want to waste any more time. "Tell me, what can an ordinary guy do to find his answers?"

"Huh!" Mr. Barco looked directly at me. His usual calm demeanor suddenly changed. His hands closed into fists, and he started shaking his head. I didn't know what I had done wrong; it was like that dreadful school afternoon all over again. However, this time the whole thing passed by as quickly as it came. Then he looked around; as if his eyes were searching for a clue. He said, "First, you have to know that there's no such thing as an ordinary guy."

I was stunned; I couldn't believe what I had heard. I accidentally blurted out in reflex, "There's no what?"

Mr. Barco didn't pay any attention to what I had said, and he continued, "I daresay you're a superpower. I hope they don't charge me with blasphemy if I say you're as powerful as god. I think the religion thing has been pushed too hard on us. Every religion is trying to prove how great its supremo is, and what kind of superpower that being possesses. Tell me how that helps a normal person connect himself with god? If anything, it creates more distance. But imagine what might happen if the search for a superpower started with us. Believe it or not, each human being is a superpower."

I didn't want to argue, but couldn't stop myself from asking, "But who is going to believe that, sir?"

"I'm coming to that," he said. "In fact, I can prove it to you right now. You see all the food lying on the tables in this restaurant? Tell me what would happen if it was left there." He smiled. "Well, you don't need to answer that. It would all go bad and start rotting and stinking after a few days. Now picture what happens when it's consumed by people instead of being left to rot: your body pulls out the nutrients from that food and releases them into your bloodstream. That food becomes the energy or the raw materials to repair and build new tissues you need to grow and move. Step-by-step, it's a very complex process, yet it's done by so-called ordinary people like you and me. Tell me, can any scientist replicate that?"

I knew there was no point in arguing. But that brought me to my next question. "If everyone has the same superpower, how do you justify one or two people coming out on top?"

"That's easy, Rohan. We all drive cars that can fly from zero to more than hundred miles an hour. But we all drive at different speeds suitable to our own needs and attitude. We all have infinite possibilities, but ultimately it depends on how much of that power we want to exert. Those with dedication, higher ambitions, and perseverance always push it to the limit."

I kept quiet. He had a compelling argument; there was no denying that fact. When I first had started working, I had exerted myself to my full capacity, and I saw results too. Well, if I had done that once, I should be able to do it again. I must forge ahead to find my answer.

I took a sip of my coffee; by then it had gone totally cold. I felt a little warm inside the restaurant, so I unbuttoned my jacket and looked up at Mr. Barco.

After a short pause, he continued. "Now tell me, if you can do all these things without even thinking, aren't you a superpower? The problem is, we keep doing all these amazing things ourselves without even knowing that we've such powers within us.

"People say it's difficult to grasp the concept of god, but that's because they've never seen god or anything like god. But if they believe the superpower thing actually starts with them, it'll be much easier to understand the concept of god rather than running to him in fear. To think of it, if one can convert food into energy, I can't think of anything that person cannot do. So, if god is all about awesome superpowers, as many religions say, then maybe each person is a little god. That person can do anything once they set their mind to it."

I loved talking to Mr. Barco; he always discussed everything on a wider canvas. He could bring personal issues to the realm of universal questions, and then show me how to consider it all from each possible viewpoint. It was much like hang gliding: experiencing and analyzing life from a dimension never seen before. Thank god I had met Mr. Barco again in Lauterbrunnen.

Chapter 7

WHEN MR. BARCO'S HALF-BROTHER left for London a few days later, Mr. Barco and Tess insisted that I move into their place. Mr. Barco assured me that he didn't have to teach for the rest of the week: "Why don't you come stay with us for the next few days, so that we can spend more time together?"

I didn't need much convincing, anyway; I was eagerly waiting for another chance to talk to him alone. I still had plenty to ask.

The Barco house looked like a nineteenth-century Impressionist painting: a small one-story cottage with slate-colored roofing tiles and big white-framed glass windows. The huge balcony overlooked blooming flowerbeds; and a nicely maintained, sprawling lawn was in front, surrounded by a white picket fence. Tess got out of the car and opened the wooden gate for us to drive in.

I was dazed; the peace and serenity all around simply overwhelmed me. I immediately thanked Mr. and Mrs. Barco for opening their home to me. I couldn't even imagine what it would be like waking up there every morning for the next few days.

After a round of tea and cookies, Tess showed me the guest room in the attic. It wasn't much; it had a comfortable bed, a cupboard, and a writing table with a chair. But that was, indeed, more than enough for me. What I liked most about the room was the view from the window. I pulled up the chair close to the window and sat there for a while, enjoying the fading sunlight from the glaciers.

The peace of mind and the comfort I enjoyed in that little room was something I hadn't experienced in a long time. In the last few years, I had never felt at home even when I was in

Uday Mukerji

my own house; I never felt close to anyone, even when I was lying next to my dearest person. There was always a distance.

After dinner, Mr. Barco said he had a surprise for me. I waited in anticipation as he took out an old photo album and showed me a few pictures of my dad—photos I never knew existed. "Those were taken a long time ago in our school days, when we were very young," he explained.

I could imagine my father being young once, but it took me a while to adjust to what I saw in those slightly fading snapshots: my dad pushing and shoving, teasing and laughing like all sixteen-year-olds do. I guess I had always pictured him as a serious schoolteacher and my dad, and had never thought of him as another kid growing-up. I held each image in my hands for as long as I could, and thanked Mr. Barco for sharing those moments with me.

Later, as I was about to head toward the attic, Mr. Barco handed me a few photographs in an envelope and said, "This is for you."

At first I didn't want to take the precious things from his collection; I knew he must've deeply cherished those pictures to have preserved them for such a long time. But he said, "Take a few; I've plenty. Let him be with you for the rest of your journey."

I couldn't say 'no' anymore. I desperately needed guidance and company; Mr. Barco and my dad had always seemed to have answers to all my problems. I quickly took the envelope from his hand and wished them good night.

Once in my room, I opened the envelope and laid out all ten photographs on my bed. I wanted to see the pictures again in absolute privacy. I suddenly felt empty inside; I missed my dad. About four months before, he had suffered a massive coronary attack six days after he retired. Who dies like that? He left us all without even saying good-bye.

I couldn't imagine how difficult it would be for Lisa and Matthew to grow up without a father by their side every day. I felt sorry for them. I would never have survived without my dad. For every question I had during my childhood, he had an answer. I always thought my father was a living encyclopedia; many times I asked him questions just to check the depth of his knowledge. My father would laugh and say, "What's this, you're my teacher now?"

I would put on his glasses and playfully answer, "Yes, I am."

"Do you know that comes with an obligation on your part?"

"What obligation, Dad?"

"If I can't answer, you have to answer the question. That's a teacher's obligation; you can't fail your student."

His voice suddenly echoed in my ears. Tears rolled down my cheeks; I felt a lump in my throat. When would I ever get used to living without him? Not that we agreed on all things in life, but we always respected each other's point of view. I looked up to my dad not for just academic knowledge; I would go to him for critical life lessons too. Funny how of all people, he was the one I called for advice after my first date with Mimi. It may sound unbelievable, but he was the only person on earth I could turn to in a crisis like that, even though it was a good crisis.

After my first super-awesome date with Mimi, when I woke up the next morning, I could still feel the taste of her kiss from the previous night. I couldn't go another minute without telling someone about what had happened the night before.

I was dying to call Mimi and express my feelings, but I wasn't sure whether that would be the right thing to do. At least my college buddies wouldn't have thought so. They went by the book when it came to dating; they would've called it a dating disaster. But if my feelings were genuine, how could it be wrong?

The dating rules on our campus were dominated by a few American and European guys who were considered the dating gurus; not because they knew any better, but because they had the most girls. But I was in no way ready to accept their rule about no calls for forty-eight hours after the first date. How stupid was that? And anyway, I didn't want to handle the situation like a college kid.

I needed advice from a mature person, so I called the one I always called in distress, or whenever I needed advice: my dad, Ravi Fernandez, a brilliant scholar and a literary person, an upright schoolteacher, and a devoted family man all his life. Although I had never talked about any of my girlfriends with him before, I knew that any advice from him would be unbiased, free from emotion, and totally logical.

I reached the McDonald's next to my dad's school long before his classes finished, and ordered an iced tea. I decided to wait at a table next to the window, so that I could see him as soon as his car showed up in the driveway.

But to my surprise my dad suddenly appeared from nowhere and said, "Hello, son!"

Although I'd had my eyes fixed on the driveway, I was so lost in my thoughts that I hadn't actually seen him coming. "Where did you park?" I asked immediately. How had I missed that? I soon collected myself and greeted my father, but I guess I still looked dazed.

My dad said, "It happens, son."

By then I was really puzzled; I had not told him anything yet. "What happens, Dad? I don't get it."

"I mean when you're in love, you don't see anything else, like what happened now," he explained.

"Who said anything about being in love? I'm not in love."

"Never mind that; tell me who this girl is. Where did you meet her?"

I told him everything—from the very minute I met Mimi at my friend's house to what had happened the night before. I spoke so fast that at times, I might have sounded a little incoherent; but I was afraid that I would miss something important if I slowed down.

"Tell me, Dad, what was it like when you first met Mom? When and how did you know that she was the right person for you?"

"I can tell you all about it, but honestly, son, no two love stories are the same. That's why whenever there is a love story published, if it's original in content it always draws people in. Each love story is unique; each person's feeling is proprietary. Moreover, your mother and I . . ." he smiled and then continued, "that was a long time ago; time has changed. Today, people have become more demanding, distrustful, and afraid of commitment. But don't worry, my son, true love is beyond all this."

"What do you mean?" I immediately put down my iced tea and leaned toward him.

"I mean that true love is honest and pure. True love doesn't allow you to play games with each other. It comes from your heart, and not from your brain. You know what, love has no logic. That's why true love isn't about winning or losing. It comes to everyone at least once in their lifetime; but most of us are too busy to notice it. We lose it or throw it away or mistakenly take it as another dating game."

Thank god I had gone to him instead of taking advice from my college buddies. He also told me to follow my heart.

"Should I call her now?" I asked, and looked up to see if I could find a public phone.

"Yes, you can. But my son, I think you should wait until I'm finished."

"You are not?"

"Don't be impatient. You'll need to give it some time for your heart to process it, to know for sure that this is love and not infatuation. And there's another important element in true love—it's a two-way street. Talk to her and find out that she feels the same way about you too. Otherwise, you may have to work on it."

Now I was confused; how does one work on such things? It wasn't anything like schoolwork, after all.

He said, "You have to impress her with qualities that other men don't have or are too afraid to exhibit; you have to show your vulnerability. This is like exposing your weaknesses to your opponent; that's of course easier said than done. But remember, only a weak fighter is afraid of disclosing his weaknesses."

The clock struck two o'clock. My dad got up from his seat and apologized that he had to leave. I assured him that he had helped me clear my thoughts; I knew what to do.

"Best of luck, son." He turned and left the restaurant.

The church clock in the tiny Alpine village sounded so real that I quickly ran to the window. It was, indeed, two o'clock in the morning. I looked outside; and the quiet Swiss village had already gone to sleep. I decided to put the pictures in my suitcase for now. I thanked my dad again for everything he had done for me, and turned off the lights.

Chapter 8

AFTER A SOUND SLEEP, the next day I woke up to the aroma of morning coffee filling the whole house. Mr. Barco and Tess were having breakfast on the balcony; but Tess came to the living room as soon as she saw me. "Good morning. Cup of coffee?"

"Yes, thank you."

"Did you sleep well?"

"Absolutely. I love the silence here."

"We love that too."

Tess had to leave for the restaurant soon, but she told me that she would be back by teatime, and she had left detailed instructions with Mr. Barco; he would prepare my breakfast and lunch.

True enough, Mr. Barco swung into action as soon as I finished my coffee. He passed me the breadbasket with cheese, and whipped out a mushroom omelet and a plate of Swiss sausages in no time. I must've been hungry. I sat there at the kitchen counter and finished everything. Then, I poured two cups of coffee—one for myself and one for my old teacher—and we both walked to the balcony to enjoy the summer sun and the view.

The mountains were so close that I could almost touch them from the balcony; the sharp rocks stood like a steep wall barely a few hundred yards away. The White Lütschine River flowed gently beyond the end of the narrow asphalt road. I could also see part of the Staubbach Falls tumbling down the cliff, and the strong wind spraying the water droplets all around.

Any other time, I would've spent hours nature gazing; but I knew my time here with Mr. Barco was very precious, and I wanted to get some definite answers from him. I needed to know what I was doing wrong, why everything I had thought right in the last twelve years suddenly looked like a gigantic mistake. Now, at thirty-six, I was like a lost kid at a carnival. What should I have done—followed up on the questions from my childhood or worked on my relationships? But I also knew it was more than my inquisitive mind that had caused the failure of my relationship with Mimi.

Now that I had Mr. Barco all to myself, I wanted to get his views as well. I briefly told him everything that had happened between Mimi and me—from our first meeting until we had officially separated about a month before. And more importantly, how our relationship had changed over time.

"Well, that's nothing new, Rohan. People change with time; that's a given in any relationship. A family tree is like any other tree – a living thing, forever growing. And while growing, its branches never pan out in the same direction; they go all over. That doesn't mean you have to cut off the branches or the whole tree. All trees learn to live with its branches going in all directions. In fact, that's the beauty of a tree; otherwise, it would've also tipped over much easily," said Mr. Barco.

"But it wasn't working, sir." I mumbled.

"What wasn't working, Rohan? Do you abandon your car if it breaks down in the middle of your journey? No, you don't; you work on it until you know that it's beyond all repair."

"Trust me, sir, I did; I lived in pain and agony for years. Along the way, we both conceded the bitter truth that our values in life were also very different. I felt compelled to look for the real thing beyond my hollow, materialistic life. I thought there could be more to life than what I had been living."

"I think you're looking at it all wrong. These two aren't necessarily conflicting interests; in life, it's not always one or the other. Otherwise, no explorer or scientist would've ever experienced love. An explorer often goes out for months and years in pursuit of their dreams; and that makes the person who they are. If their girlfriend or boyfriend, wife or husband truly loves them, they happily join in their partner's pursuits, or they wait behind patiently."

Mr. Barco paused and looked at his empty coffee mug. Any other time, I would've run to get him a refill; but I was glued to the conversation.

He continued, "You can, indeed, embrace both. But instead of keeping your partner in the dark, you must trust the other person and let her into your thoughts. Remember, trust is the most important element in love. The two people in any relationship come from two different families with different backgrounds and values. Their perspectives are sure to differ. And when perspectives differ, the chance of conflict is much higher. But conflict doesn't kill relationships, conceit does. Trust builds tolerance; if we trust the other person instead of always disagreeing, we can agree to disagree. That helps us keep the channels of communication open instead of shutting them down."

True, our tolerance level had fallen to the bottom. So was it conceit that killed our relationship? But I was sure there was more. "That may be true, sir; but don't you think our modern lifestyle makes us less forgiving and more self-centered?"

"You are right, Rohan; the main problem today is the lack of tolerance. It's visible not only in a husband and wife relationship; it's everywhere. The world is becoming more and more self-centered. And it all starts at the beginning. We are constantly teaching our children how to excel, how to outperform, how to win, and how to become number one. The problem is that there's only one place on top; we aren't teaching our kids how to handle well a number two or number three position. We aren't telling them how to share, how to care for others, and how to help others in distress and destitution. So everyone grows up thinking their interests must come first. Don't forget that it's a human instinct to be selfish, like when we try to save ourselves first in extreme situations. But adding fuel to that is unthinkable."

I couldn't agree more. I had never wanted Matthew and Lisa to win number one spot at any cost. If it happened naturally, that was one thing; otherwise, living should be fun, and not a competition. I looked him in the eye and asked, "But what made us so self-centered now?"

"Well, we all are to blame for this, Rohan. Think about it; as a newborn baby, you don't have any ego. The question is, when do you get it, and from where? As you grow up, your mother tells you that you're beautiful; you grow up believing you're good-looking. You don't know you're efficient until your boss appreciates your work, or you receive commendation letters. You don't know you're kind unless your friends tell you so, or you're honored for your charity work. It's the society that builds and fuels your ego.

"I admit being number one is good. But what's so humiliating in being number two? What's the time difference between the one who clocks first and the one who clocks second in a sprint, or in an Olympic swimming competition? Not much, right? When two boxers enter a ring, shouldn't we cheer for both of them for being brave? When one wins, the other boxer has to lose; and there's no shame in that. In fact, we should celebrate the second-place boxer's bravery and courage for being there all alone against that formidable champion. But in society, we often celebrate the successful individuals, and not their performances or achievements. We show no appreciation at all for the rest. Only the winner becomes a celebrity. And now, see what people are doing to become one."

I understood what he meant by celebrating individuals and not the quality of the performances. There was a time when you needed real talent to achieve fame; now you could be famous for no reason at all. But I also knew that there was a big world beyond that; and many successful people deserved their fame. I asked, "In reality, can fame be such a bad thing, sir?"

"The point is, fame isn't bad if it's treated as a delightful extra, like adding chili sauce to French fries. But unfortunately, to many it works like an addiction. If the craving for fame isn't controlled or channeled in the right direction, it can land a person on the wrong side of the fence. Then, they might crave fame at any cost."

Mr. Barco took out his glasses and leaned back in his seat. "You know what, our society is changing very fast. You have to constantly filter your judgments based on what is right or wrong, and make your decisions accordingly."

"But don't you think right or wrong is a matter of perspective, sir?"

"Absolutely, Rohan; but still there may be another way to look at your life—from a distance without being a party to it— much like how you saw Lauterbrunnen while paragliding. Obviously, you can't have any idea of how big or small a place is by standing at one particular spot. But the moment you took yourself out of the map, and saw the whole area from the top, that gave you a more complete picture of the valley. And you got clarity. We often look at life in pieces, because we get too involved with momentary happiness. But if you can detach yourself from your life that will give you clarity, and help you put situations in perspective."

Is that the reason we make so many mistakes in life? Like Ade's jigsaw puzzle, we're always dealing with one piece at a time, and we never get to see the complete picture. I wanted to know if it was really possible, though, to lead a normal life and yet watch it from a distance as Mr. Barco said.

He was about to continue, but suddenly we were distracted by the sound of cowbells in the distance. I followed his eyes out to the narrow, deserted street and saw a man in a yellow jumpsuit steering his cattle back home. Mr. Barco jumped up. "That's Daniel; he always comes back home at a quarter after one from the field to go join his afternoon shift. Tess will kill me; I haven't served your lunch yet."

I tried to appease him. "Don't worry, sir. I'm not hungry anyway."

"You don't know Tess; she is very particular about guests. If she finds out I was unmindful, she'll be very upset."

He immediately rushed to the kitchen. I followed him and asked whether I could help, but Mr. Barco shook his head. He showed me a wooden stool in front of the kitchen counter, asked me to sit down, and instead tell him how my mother was doing.

To think of it, I myself didn't know how she was doing. I hadn't asked her that in a long time. My dad had passed away in the middle of a chaotic time for me. Although we all met at the funeral, I had been so busy struggling with my marriage and some important life questions of my own that I failed to carry out the most basic duty to my mother.

Imagine what happens to a revolving carousel when its z-axis suddenly breaks down in the middle of a busy carnival. I guess the same thing happened to my mother; but I was too selfish to see it. My mother's life had always revolved around my dad's world. It wasn't because she couldn't do anything else; she had chosen to give up everything to concentrate on her family, which was more precious to her. As far back as I could remember, I had always seen her as a housewife and a mother; but my dad told us that she was a very good student, even better than he was. She was also a good painter; but all those things meant nothing to her once they decided to get married and my sister and I were born.

What made her give up everything—her career, her future? I had never seen her sad or never thought she had ever regretted those decisions. My parents stayed married without any complaint; and they always looked genuinely happy. It was so unlike the marriages in our generation. What is it that they were doing right and we're screwing up?

I guess it boils down to sacrifice and tolerance, like Mr. Barco said. We love our partners; but we love ourselves more. We always put ourselves first, while they did exactly the opposite. They did everything in their power to make their other half succeed and shine; and to do that, they often sacrificed their own career and wishes. They took happiness in their partner's glory; they felt good being able to give something to a person who needed it more. That didn't make them any less of an achiever, or weak or unhappy—in fact, quite the opposite. Imagine being able to give food to one who's hungry, or medicine to someone sick, or guidance to someone lost, or simply money to someone poor; that doesn't make one any less affluent. If anything, it makes the giver stronger. But as Mr. Barco said, these qualities are fast fading from the society; we're left with nothing but false pride and self-interest.

Had I really taken my mother's love and care for granted? My mother had never seemed to care about her personal needs; she did everything to make us happy. That's why she broke down after my dad's death. She was all alone there. She even told me that she wanted to leave Singapore and move back to Goa. I didn't understand 'why'; so I didn't give it much thought.

I guess my silence spoke volumes. Mr. Barco must've sensed that I didn't have any good answers for him. After setting the table, he looked at me and said, "I know you were close to your dad; maybe it's time you got close to your mother."

Since we were on the subject, I thought it would be good to get Mr. Barco's view on why my mother suddenly wanted to go back to Goa after living in Singapore for nineteen years.

"Have you ever considered that it might not be such a bad idea?"

I couldn't believe what I had heard. "But we all live in Singapore; there's no one in Goa. Who'll look after her?"

"May I speak with you freely, Rohan?"

I nodded.

"Isn't that a selfish thought? You're only thinking of your inconvenience if she ever fell sick in Goa. Shouldn't you think this through from her point of view as well?"

I realized Mr. Barco was right; I was only considering the relocation from my angle. She had lost her life partner—in fact, she'd lost everything. How does one cope with that? She never spoke much; but since my dad passed away, she had spoken even less.

I asked, "What shall I do? ... Maybe I can talk to her as soon as I go back to Singapore, and see what she wants."

Mr. Barco smiled. "That would be a good start, Rohan."

I felt much better. I loved my mom dearly; and I sincerely wanted to see her happy again. Now that my dad was gone, the responsibility was definitely on me.

Why hadn't I thought of this before? Why did I keep ignoring her calls and voice messages? As it is, she had never called unless there was something important; she wasn't one of those pestering mothers. She was, indeed, a strong woman inside, maybe one of the strongest I had ever seen. I choked up and quickly ran to the bathroom. I washed my face a couple of times, but hesitated to look up and see my face in the mirror. I remembered a lesson I had learned from her: "If you're true to yourself, you'll never be afraid to see your face in the mirror," she used to say.

Like my dad, my mother had always made serious life lessons very simple for us. While Goa may not be the best place on earth to raise children, she gave us a lot of freedom. She never believed in watching over our shoulders. She always had one piece of advice: "Do anything and everything you like; but don't do anything that you have to avoid talking about when you come back home."

That line had both haunted and guided me throughout my life. Even at a young age, I had understood that when the burden of choosing right from wrong was left on me, I must be extra careful.

Now I could confidently say that I wouldn't have been me without her. I looked up in the mirror, water still dripping from my face. "Sorry, Mom," I murmured, and I reached for a towel.

Chapter 9

AN HOUR LATER, I found Mr. Barco on the balcony relaxing in his armchair with his eyes closed. I quietly pulled another chair closer to him. By then the afternoon sun had moved to the west. Much of the valley had already lost the warmth of the summer sun for the day. The tower clock at the village church struck four. Mr. Barco opened his eyes and smiled.

I said, "I can't thank you enough, sir, for your hospitality and your advice."

"I'm glad you liked it here, son." He looked out into the open valley.

The more I saw that man, the more intrigued I became. He always seemed calm and composed; he never looked worried about anything. Did he honestly have access to the complete picture of the jigsaw puzzle of his life? It brought me back to our unfinished conversation before lunch.

It would, indeed, be nice to see my whole life in perspective all the time. I also would've loved to see all my jigsaw pieces and the full picture behind the box. Then, I could possibly help Adeline, too. I began to wonder whether what Mr. Barco was about to reveal might help me plan the rest of my journey and my search; so I asked him to continue.

Mr. Barco began, "Well, let me tell you how one can live life without getting too involved. Think of your life as an act in a play, and you're an actor in it. Now if you're playing the role of a homeless guy, do you ever feel sorry for yourself? If you play the role of a super-rich business tycoon, do you go on a spending spree? I don't think so. Similarly, if you could look at your life as acting in a play, you would perform your role to the best of your ability, without being really sad or happy. Because all this is just a play; and you're only playing your role. The idea is to live life from the outside as a spectator, and not to get too involved in it. This allows you to see things more objectively and be detached from the materialistic world. It'll automatically make life less complicated and will give you more control over your actions."

Maybe Mimi and I could've avoided most of our bitter arguments if I had sincerely played the role of a busy executive without thinking too much about myself, and concentrated more on the role itself. Could I have done that? But I was puzzled about one thing: "If role playing is all life is about, what happens to ambition and motivation?"

"I don't see any conflict there, Rohan. If you're an ambitious guy, you might still want to be the best role player. If you've a small part today as a homeless guy, one day, don't you want to grab the role of the young hero who saves the life of a beautiful girl and gets to kiss her every day onstage? Ambition is a good thing, but it becomes ugly when it blinds you to everything but achieving it."

Indeed, living that way would make things much less complicated. But how does one do that? Was I supposed to put myself in the audience chair now and watch Rohan play the role of a confused guy? I would've loved to watch that show.

Tess showed up at the main gate, and I came back to my senses. "It must be past five," said Mr. Barco. We both stood to greet Tess; and Mr. Barco went inside to make tea. Tess put down her bag on the side table and sat next to me.

She must be in her late forties, I thought, though her sharp features and short hair made her look much younger. She had an air of elegance; poise, finesse, and confidence radiated from every move she made. In the prime of her career, she had left the corporate world for good when her company wanted to move her to its Chicago office. Instead, Mr. and Mrs. Barco had opted for a quieter life in Lauterbrunnen. Tess had opened a small café, and Mr. Barco had taken a part-time teaching job in Interlaken. She hired a very efficient, energetic waitress who also doubled up as a cashier. They split the work between them such that Tess could always come back home at a decent time.

We sat there in silence until Mr. Barco returned ten minutes later with steaming-hot tea and homemade cookies. He put down the tray, and Tess took over from there. The aroma of the beautiful Darjeeling tea filled the air.

"These cookies are excellent. When do you find time to bake and do all the cooking?" I asked.

"I do the bare minimum. You must've noticed that we don't need much. Both of us believe in simple living. In fact, that's what drew me to this schoolteacher once." She reached for Mr. Barco's hand, and she smiled; I would've loved to know the secrets behind the success of that marriage.

After taking a small sip from her teacup, Tess said, "It all happened twenty years ago. Joseph and I first met at an art exhibition in Goa. A week later, when my friends left for Zurich, I decided to stay back for few more days. As I was roaming the streets of Panjim on my own, I accidentally lost my wallet. I had no money, no passport, and nobody to turn to in a foreign land. Fortunately, I remembered where he worked. So, I called Joseph Barco. He showed up in exactly twenty-two minutes; I remember it well because I was counting every minute that day. And from that moment onward, I never felt alone, ever. I was impressed the first time he invited me to his place. He immediately took me to his house and offered his only bedroom to me. I objected and volunteered to take the couch instead. But he insisted. You know what he said? 'This is Indian hospitality. I swear I'm not doing anything special for you that any other Indian wouldn't have done for his guests. This is our philosophy in life; now that you're in India, please accept it the Indian way.' And I knew he was the one."

I bet Tess had learned quite a bit from that experience; her hospitality was both genuine and heartwarming. She had made me feel at home the moment I stepped into that Swiss haven. I was thoroughly enjoying the heavenly peace of Lauterbrunnen

village and the great company of Tess and Joseph Barco. I
hadn't felt this comfortable in a long time. I also hadn't felt the
tumultuous waves breaking in my head since I had moved in
here. It was certainly the effect of the Barco family
atmosphere. It allowed me to think clearly.

However, that was cut short when I received a call from
my daughter later in the evening. Lisa wanted to know whether
I would be back in time to attend her birthday party. I didn't
have the heart to disappoint her. The fact is, in the middle of
all that was going on, I was hesitant to see Mimi again.

But how could I ignore the birthday of my own daughter?
Unforgivable; I couldn't believe it. Wasn't I the most self-
centered person in the whole world? Hadn't I learned anything
from Mr. Barco? I couldn't jeopardize my kids' happiness
because I was in the middle of a crisis myself. As Mr. Barco
said, I must learn to live with both. I needed to put his words
into practice and see where that would lead me.

I didn't want to miss Lisa's birthday under any
circumstances, Hence, the next morning, I called the airline,
booked an evening flight back to Singapore, packed my bag,
and headed to the Lauterbrunnen railway station. I was happy
that I had met Mr. Barco again and his wife, Tess; and I
thanked them both for making me feel at home for the first
time in a long while.

Mr. Barco wanted to drive me to the station. "It's only a
five- to seven-minute drive."

As he drove the car out of the main gate, I stood outside
taking one last look at the beautiful cottage in front of the
gigantic rocks. I had a lot on my mind. The present looked
confusing; the future, bleak. Before I had gotten married, my
problems were strictly mine; any decision then would've only
impacted me. But not anymore.

I didn't know which decision to address first. I felt I
couldn't live another day without knowing my role in the
universe. My career path looked dead, and so did my

relationships. In the last few days, I had received a lot of help from Mr. Barco; but obviously he couldn't make a decision for me. I had to settle my personal dilemmas myself.

As we came closer to the railway station, my fear of losing him again became more acute. Here, at least, I could get his opinion on everything; but once I left Lauterbrunnen, I would be completely on my own again. If I had to ask any last-minute question, now would be the time before we reached the railway station. In spite of sounding desperate and incoherent, I said, "At times, I feel nothing is working out for me; I'm so overwhelmed." I fell short of saying that he should simply tell me what to do—though I wished he would.

Mr. Barco calmly said, "Then it's time you pulled out your life chart. You know, Rohan, in life one cannot avoid disasters or bad times. However, one can always reduce the force of that blow. A good way to do that is to keep a scorecard of all the good and bad things that have happened to you since your early childhood. Write down each time your prayer has been answered and you were rewarded with more than you wanted; and side by side, also make a list of every single time your prayer was declined, or you thought you didn't get what you deserved in life. You have to do this list very carefully; count every close shave and all undue gains. Chances are we all have received more favors than rejections. Ask anyone; possibly ninety-five percent of our wishes have come true. The unfortunate part is, we all overlook that, and regret all our lives and torment ourselves for not getting the other five percent."

By then, we had reached the station and started walking toward the platform. I hauled my luggage and stayed close to him. I didn't want to miss a thing.

He continued, "So, whenever you're going through a bad time or you're about to face an imminent loss of money, job, health, or anything at all, you need to pull out the overall scorecard and check how many times the scale has tipped in your favor."

I could suddenly see my last few months spread out on a postmortem table. True enough, my marriage hadn't worked out, and my career was at a crossroads, but I couldn't deny that I also had gotten my fair share of wishes granted. I had lived a healthy life, had received a good education, had a great job, and I was blessed with two great kids.

"So, what do I do next?" I asked.

"You do nothing; live your life as usual. If you're disillusioned with your life, and you question what you've done or achieved in all these years, then, my son, I would like you to look at those who are living their lives with a lot less than what you have. Their numbers are many times higher than those who have more to squander. And even with so little to live with, they haven't lost the smiles on their faces."

"But don't we all want to reach our goals in life?"

"Of course we do. But unfortunately life is made of several goalposts, and not one. As we grow up and reach our first goal in life, we shift our goalpost with new and higher ambition. My guess is that when you got married, your goal shifted to making more money and having an affluent lifestyle. And after fulfilling that, now you're looking for new goals. That's all."

Indeed, he was right; my priorities had changed between then and now. It clearly explained the void; of course, when we shift from one field to another for a new game, we all need time to acclimatize ourselves. "But how do I know that I'll achieve my goal now?"

Mr. Barco answered calmly, "Simply put, you don't. And that's life; you have to keep working at it. All you can do is take your best shot; living is an attitude, Rohan. And making a difference doesn't mean having more money or more fame than others. It would be unwise to think that your life or profession doesn't make any difference because there're a million other people living next to you doing the same thing. The fact is, a janitor's contribution is no less important than a scientist's work, because a scientist wouldn't be able to carry out their lab work if the janitor didn't clean the lab; the lab would be contaminated.

"Can you say which one is any less or any more important than the other? You can feel miserable and spend every single day feeling sorry for yourself, or you can do your work with passion, feel great, and live every minute of your life. The choice is always yours."

As much as I wanted to believe him, I knew that I was worse than a janitor; I had no passion left for my job or for my life. I felt frustrated and tired. I asked Mr. Barco what would happen if at any point a person became disinterested in life and decided to stay away from his passions.

Mr. Barco shook his head and then looked at me. "How do you expect to find your connection by not being connected? You must know one thing about the universe: it stops for no one, and stops at nothing. Not accepting life is like boycotting the obvious. Imagine an occasion like Christmas or a celebration like New Year's Eve; the party will go on with you or without you. It doesn't matter whether you participate or not. You can always watch it on TV, or go down and join in the festivities."

A bright yellow narrow-gage train to Interlaken Ost was already waiting at the platform. As the signal changed, I hugged Mr. Barco and boarded the train. Mr. Barco waved. The train chugged along its track, leaving beautiful green Alpine meadows on both sides. In the distance, snow-capped mountains smiled as the sunlight reflected on them. Beautiful small cottages dotted the mountain slopes. Unfortunately, I wasn't looking at any of those; my mind was still occupied with the last few days' conversations with Mr. Barco.

Chapter 10

I CHANGED TRAINS at Interlaken and reached Zurich in the early evening. I knew it would be a long flight to Singapore; thank god I had an aisle seat. I stretched my feet out. Once the flight took off, the hustle and bustle inside the airplane died down immediately. As I settled myself comfortably in my seat, the wedding ring on my finger suddenly caught my eye. Oh my god! Why was it still there?

I couldn't be seen wearing this in Singapore. Unsuccessfully, I tried a couple of times to pull it off my ring finger; finally, I had to go into the bathroom to apply soap and water to remove it. However, it left a conspicuous tan line. Of course, how could ten years of a relationship vanish without a trace?

My ring finger looked ugly with that pale round white mark. Although I didn't want to take a second look, I couldn't keep my eyes off it. I examined my fingers from both front and back; it looked ridiculous, but there was nothing I could do to remove the tan line.

As I stretched out my hand yet again, it must've caught the attention of the woman sitting next to me. "Pretty recent, huh?" she asked.

"Excuse me?" I glanced at her; she was half smiling. But there was also a concerned look in her eyes. She was an elegant woman, maybe in her early forties. I first thought she was a tourist, but she corrected me immediately and said, "I'm going to work in Singapore. By the way, I'm Claire."

"Rohan," I said, introducing myself. "But honestly, how do you know?"

"With that obvious tan line, it couldn't have been long."

"About a month...but I took off the ring today."

She smiled. "You wasted a month."

"Pardon me?" I felt curious to know what she meant.

"Don't forget you won't heal completely until that tan line is gone. It works as a constant reminder. Slowly but surely it'll go away; you gotta give it time."

"You sure know a lot about ring tan lines."

"You can say that." She held out her left hand for me to take a closer look, though I wasn't quite sure what I was looking at. It was perfectly manicured; there was no wedding ring or tan line.

She said, "I was married for eight years. And then, boom! Suddenly one day it was all over. Don't worry, everything fades with time." And she looked out the window.

I sincerely hoped so. For a moment I thought of Adeline. She must've noticed that ring too; nothing slipped past her eyes. Amazing! She hadn't mentioned it, not even once, whereas even my fellow passenger seemed curious. I told Ade that my marriage was over; but she had never asked me anything? Maybe it hadn't bothered her; but I also didn't think Ade was that frivolous type who would say 'I love you' to a married man. Or had she felt confident enough to ignore the ring, knowing it would all come out in due time? Indeed, that woman's mind was a maze.

I must've dozed off for a while after dinner. When I woke up it was quite dark; only the nightlights were on inside the airplane. I looked outside, but nothing much was visible except the flickering wing lights. I pulled down the blind and closed my eyes again.

As I woke up in the morning, I headed for the bathroom. Claire was right; every time I looked at my right hand, it invariably reminded me of incidents from my married life.

The thought of Mimi as my ex-wife sent chills through my veins. It was like suddenly I had lost a limb. The closer I came to Singapore, the emptier I felt. It would be my first visit after finalizing our divorce, and like it or not, I knew things would be different.

When I had taken off about a month before, I was in pain, and I was even more confused. My knee-jerk reaction was one of anger and self-pity. It seemed as though after my dad's death, everything had happened in a domino effect: I decided to pursue my search for a real purpose of existence, Mimi and I had finally liberated ourselves, and I took a long leave from my job to make up my mind—about everything.

But as time passed, I had slowly gotten hold of myself. Spending time with Mr. Barco had showed me new ways to deal with my problems. Now, I could admit that what had happened in the last six months was the cumulative effect of the last nineteen years.

Since my family had moved to Singapore nineteen years before in search of a better life, a lot had changed. While growing up in India, I had hardly known that I was missing out on life, simply because I hadn't seen anything in life yet. But once we came to Singapore, I realized that my dad had barely been able to make ends meet. Initially, he couldn't even afford a car; he used to take public transportation to work. The first generation of immigrants always bears the brunt of the hardship. My parents were working hard to keep the family afloat.

I felt bad that I wasn't able to do anything to help out. A scholarship would've definitely eased the financial pressure. But with my poor grades, I was lucky to even get accepted to a college program. That made me realize: all doors are closed to anyone average. I became more focused and serious in college, and managed to get a place in a coveted MBA Program at the National University of Singapore. And as I finished my MBA, I met Mimi—a beautiful Chinese girl worth pursuing.

Our first meeting was at a friend's party in Singapore. My final exam was over and I was looking for any excuse to party, but it wasn't a fancy event—just one of those usual college house parties, with lots of booze and real loud music. Although at first, things were pretty formal, after a few hours of nonstop chatting and a few rounds of shots, we felt quite drawn to each other. However, to prove that it wasn't the alcohol that had brought us closer, we decided to do dinner the very next day.

I would never forget how I scrambled for money that day. But the truth is, it was the best date I'd had in my life.

We went to Holland Village for dinner. Mimi was looking gorgeous in tight, torn blue jeans and a halter-neck top with high-heeled shoes. She had shoulder-length dark hair and silky, smooth skin. In sum, she was the kind we all feared and desired the most. If I had seen her anywhere else—in a library or in a pub—I would've avoided even making an eye contact, let alone saying 'hello'. So, did I feel a little proud parading her from the parking lot to the restaurant? Well, maybe a little. Who wouldn't have been? People were looking at us—though mostly at her.

That day it all felt so different. As we settled comfortably inside the restaurant, Mimi did most of the talking; I sat there quietly. It was all as engrossing as a children's storybook, where the princess lives happily ever after. As she kept reading pages from her life, I sat there watching her. She told me a lot of things; some I listened to and remembered, and others got lost in my daydreaming. Mimi's grandfather had come to Singapore in the 1930s from a small town in Shandong Province in eastern China. He had started a small garment factory, but it soon closed down during the Japanese occupation.

But her father didn't want to give up on that business idea. He borrowed money in order to introduce a full line of bedding collections, and with his hard work and business acumen, that venture paid off. Mimi didn't really experience any of their family hardship; she grew up in luxury and opulence. Mimi was the only child in the family and got everything she wanted before she could even ask. Her mother was a traditional Chinese Singaporean and had worked in a bank for a good part of her life. However, her parents had recently moved to operate out of Hong Kong.

Soon a waiter showed up, handed over the dinner and cocktail menu, "Anything to drink, sir?"

I looked at Mimi, and asked, "Wine?"

Mimi didn't even look at the wine card; she wanted to leave everything to me that night.

I felt a little intimidated at first. I had no clue how to order wine for myself, let alone for a girl like that. One wrong step and I might be out of the race. Was this a test or what?

"Red or white?" I tried to narrow down her choices.

"I don't mind red, if you're okay with that."

I looked up at the waiter and ordered a bottle of slightly expensive Pinot Noir. I thought price should be a good indicator of quality.

During the dinner, Mimi told me more stories from her school days: about her dog, Coco who had died about two years earlier, and her best friend, Laura. Mimi and Laura had been best friends since the first day at school. Naturally, when Laura's Tibetan spaniel, Sasha gave birth to five puppies in their freshman year of high school, Mimi had gotten one of them; and that gave them more reasons to see each other every day. Although Mimi had gone off to New South Wales University for four years in Sydney, she and Laura had stayed in touch. When Mimi came back, the friendship grew even closer.

Mimi had started off her career at her dad's new company—a spinoff to sell online their own products and other labels as well. I remembered thinking that her dad had made an excellent choice by hiring Mimi; she was smart, intelligent, persuasive, and ambitious. I was sure any company would've been lucky to have her at the helm.

We were so engrossed in each other that I didn't remember anything about the food. Anyway, restaurant food is never just about the food; it's the sum of food, ambience, and service.

Every time all three pieces are put together in perfect harmony, fine dining is born.

After dinner, as we walked back to the public parking lot, Mimi asked me, "How about a simple dessert?"

I was confused; I stopped in the middle of the road. Hadn't she said 'no' minutes before, when I asked her inside the restaurant? I looked at her bewildered.

"I know. I know. But this gotta be my treat!"

Opposite the parking lot there was a Haagen-Dazs restaurant. We first looked at the restaurant, then at each other, and started walking in that direction. Lucky thing, it wasn't too crowded that night. We got a window-side table.

"What's dinner without dessert?" I said.

Mimi couldn't agree more. "I simply wanted to say thanks with a token of appreciation. Hope you don't mind."

"Of course not. This is great. But what I don't understand is why you're in such a hurry to thank me."

"In case you don't call me again. You can never be too sure about this dating stuff."

"I doubt that'll happen here."

"We'll see about that."

After finishing dessert, we both felt like we had overeaten. I suggested that we could walk it off at the East Coast Beach if she wasn't too tired; I didn't want that evening to end, at least not yet. Fortunately, Mimi loved the idea. I felt assured and relieved; she must've liked my company too.

We soon reached the East Coast Park. Mimi and I got out of the car and walked side by side toward the sea. The beach was quiet at that hour. The sound of the waves was never loud on Singapore beaches; it was more like a gentle caress of the water on the shore. The ships across the water were waiting in line for their turn at the port—in a truly disciplined Singapore style. From a distance, it looked as if the lights on the freighters were chained to one another from one corner of the east to the west as far as we could see. But the best thing about that place was the view of the incoming flights. Every five or ten minutes the strong headlights of an airplane would light up the water below, as if a space shuttle was about to descend on Singapore shores.

We barely had walked two hundred yards down the beach before I noticed that Mimi was having difficulty walking in her high heels; but she said nothing. Pointing to an empty bench, I asked, "Shall we sit there?"

Mimi jumped at the suggestion and immediately started walking in that direction.

"Why didn't you tell me?" I asked.

"Tell you what?"

"That you're having difficulty walking?"

"Nah, it was nothing. I didn't want to un-impress you. Besides, I can't be any shorter than I already am. Anyway, how do you know? You're a mind reader, aren't you?"

"You know what, you can never un-impress me. Besides, you're about five-five, right? That's about average."

"Who said I wanted average? I hate anything average."

I should've guessed that. Indeed, there was nothing average about her. She was only twenty-two and had been living a hotshot corporate life as the vice president of strategy and planning at her dad's company. She was intelligent and ambitious. She lived alone in a sprawling house and drove a BMW. I wished I could retract my statement. But my thoughts suddenly froze as her fingers slipped into mine and I felt a chilling sensation rush from my fingers to my brain. Her hand was a bit cold, but I loved the feeling. Her skin was smooth and silky-soft, like rose petals.

It was an enchanting evening, one right out of any romance novel. The beach was exceptionally clean and nicely manicured, and it was a balmy night; the summer breeze was ruffling the palm trees and the sky was clear. Time passed like a rolling stone on a downward slope. Soon, the beach became even quieter, the side road looked deserted, and the lights in the high-rise apartments behind us turned off one by one. We didn't notice any of that. Who had time for trivialities? In the distance a church bell struck midnight. We couldn't believe our ears. We had been so absorbed in each other that two hours had gone by in a flash.

We slowly walked back to the car and thanked each other for a great time. Ten minutes later I pulled up at Mimi's house; I got out of the driver's seat, opened her door, and walked her to the doorstep. Fortunately, there was no awkward moment. Mimi leaned forward, I tilted my head slightly to the left, and we kissed passionately.

I went to bed that night completely dazed. I didn't even remember when our lips unlocked or when and how I drove back home.

Suddenly, I heard loud knocks at the bathroom door. I must've been there too long. I quickly answered, "In a minute," splashed more water on my face, and walked to my seat.

When a flight attendant came by a short while later, I ordered a cup of coffee and looked out the window. It was clear blue sky all around. I looked at my watch; it still was on Vienna time. I remembered Adeline's innocent face the last time I had seen her in my bed. She was sleeping comfortably, wrapped up in blankets. I had already packed the night before; I didn't even wake her up to say good-bye.

Now I felt terrible about it. I definitely needed to make amends.

My eyes were still fixed on my watch. This particular Tag Heuer had been my favorite since Mimi gave it to me on our first month anniversary. I was a little embarrassed at first, as I had not bought her anything. But what she said had relieved me a lot: "You've your whole life to make up for it. You're going to start work in a big office now; you need a nice watch."

With my newfound motivation I worked hard to get to the top of the corporate ladder in an attempt to see an early success that others couldn't dare. My hard work armed me with a salary and bonus that most people my age could only dream of; and I was flying high. My confidence grew by the day, and soon, I had power I had never experienced before: the power of money. The feeling was incredible. I was hooked at the first taste. It was more like a drug to me—left me intoxicated, craving more. I could access any club or any restaurant, anytime—no lines, no questions asked.

I had been focused since I first came to Singapore, but when I started working, I became obsessed. I told myself it was the only recipe for success. One gotta be obsessed with something to be the best. Einstein was obsessed. Van Gogh was obsessed.

I knew I was no genius, so I must be twice as obsessed. I might have to work twice as hard to achieve the goal I had set for myself. Of course, my goal then was very different: to stand out as one of the best fund managers, to earn a lot of money, and above all, to make Mimi happy. There was no room for complacency in my business. Even if I didn't lose a client to one of my competitors, there was every possibility that I might lose them to one of my colleagues. I did everything I could to outperform my coworkers. I quickly moved from a financial analyst job to portfolio management. I worked day and night to find success, and that hard work paid off, translating into a quarter-million-dollar bonus in the first year, and close to half a million in the second. And it kept growing. My bosses thought I was a financial genius. I received commendation letters almost every month from our offices all over the world.

I was convinced that the rulebook in life was very different for ordinary people and those who wanted to soar high. In management classes, we had learned how knowing the weaknesses allowed one to minimize losses by retreating when necessary. But after I started working, I thought this rule might be only good for those who were ordinary and wanted to play it safe in life; in reality, it would hold me back from taking risks and exploring new options. In other words, I was convinced that knowing one's weaknesses was like knowing one's limitations. Like Steve Prefontaine, those who aspired to more in life never retreated. Of course, they failed and got hurt a few times, but they reached their goals when they persevered. That's why the world often looked at them as obsessive. They knew only one way—the way forward.

However, each one of my successes came with a price tag. My carefree old school days were long gone; and after my marriage, I had hardly any time of my own. Every minute of my life seemed chained to a running wheel, mechanical and regimented—always controlled by another person. One by one, all my old friends disappeared, and before I knew it we started moving in a totally different crowd. In my college days, anyone with a common interest could've been my friend. With many different friends, I had spent countless evenings watching soccer games or movies, playing video games, drinking beer and singing karaoke. After our marriage, Mimi and I essentially had three other couple friends in our close circle, the only thing common being they were all accomplished and ambitious. Nevertheless, they were fun; or should one say intoxicating? The group was really tight, and we used to do everything together. Our weekends were packed with parties and the occasional drive to villages and sea beaches in Malaysia.

At times, though, I felt I was sliding, and my new, Singaporean materialistic values and aspirations was undermining my childhood principles and goals in life. Hard work and an honest living looked so ordinary. I wanted more. I had to convince myself that these were the small prices one had to pay for success. There was no looking back.

"More coffee, sir?" The flight attendant was standing next to me, smiling and holding a coffee pot in her hand.

"No, thank you," I said in reflex; though it took me a while to connect the dots and remember where I was. My body was definitely above 38,000 feet and maybe miles away from Singapore, but my mind had already touched down at Changi Airport. I looked at my watch, and adjusted it to Singapore time. It would be possibly another hour or so.

However, it became the longest hour of the flight. My anxiety intensified. Would Matthew and Lisa love me the same after all that had happened between Mimi and me? Would my absence for one month have made any difference? How would Mimi like my presence on Lisa's birthday? I hadn't spoken with her since I had left Singapore. I had chosen not to verify Lisa's invitation. Our conversations in the recent past had always ended up in ruthless heated arguments, and I was too tired to do that dance again. Lisa was my daughter too; I must've every right to attend her birthday. Besides, I was also desperate to see them. What would she do, stop me?

Chapter 11

SWEET HOME, SINGAPORE. The plane landed exactly on time, and I jumped into a cab to go to my new temporary home—a serviced apartment.

Although when we separated, Mimi had told me that I could come and see Matthew and Lisa anytime I wanted, I thought I had to talk to them and explain the new arrangement. Mimi and I were grown-ups; we knew what to expect. But kids often suffer the worst casualties in a divorce. I had to find a way around that. Ignoring the situation certainly wouldn't help; so I decided to take it head on, and tell them the truth every step of the way.

I drove to the house in the early afternoon to spend time with Matthew and Lisa before the party. I had never imagined that one day I would be a guest in my own home when we had bought the house about ten years before. I guess there is a first time for everything. I didn't know how to handle the simplest things. Should I park inside like I used to, or park outside like a guest? I deliberated for a moment, then parked outside on the main road and stood there thinking for a while.

The house didn't look anything like this when we first bought it; but it was still very pretty back then. In spite of our best efforts, we hadn't been able to find anything to Mimi's liking before our wedding; so we had rented a nice semi-detached house, and after coming back from our honeymoon we had zeroed in on the house hunting again. But soon the whole thing became a strain on both of us.

Those days, I didn't understand why Mimi didn't like any of the houses the brokers showed us. Those places all looked good to me: they all had two or three bedrooms, a hall, and a kitchen and dining area; and often they had balconies too. Flooring was either carpeted or parquet. What was there not to like? But now, after so many years, I finally understood why. In life, before we meet a person, see a house, or go on vacation, we create a mental picture of the subject. This conception takes shape long before the actual seeing occurs; and as time goes by, we fill the picture in with more detail until it slowly becomes a matter of obsession. The closer what we see matches our picture, the better we feel; anything else becomes unacceptable. The same thing must've happened with Mimi's house hunting. She must've had a picture of our future home in her mind, and nothing matched.

Nearly after two and a half months of house hunting, there came a breakthrough one weekend. While out jogging, she spotted a new 'For Sale' sign in the front yard of one of the houses in our neighborhood. It was a lovely two-story house with both front yard and a backyard. She immediately came back home, woke me up, and dragged me to that house—all within thirty minutes.

Mimi had always been persuasive, and she managed to convince the owners why we would be the best buyers to take care of their prized family treasure. Of course, house sellers in that economy would've been happy to get any offer at all, so Mimi won. As for me, I wanted a house, wanted it done. And from that day on, we'd had this address, and we both loved it.

Bit by bit we gave the old house a complete makeover, though it was more of Mimi's effort than mine. In close to three months' time, she carefully removed all traces of the previous owners, and made it look like an affluent young family abode. We remodeled the worn-out garage with automatic doors, but we retained the doors and window frames of the house, because they were made of solid maple and oak wood. The roofing needed a lot of work, so we changed the front porch roof totally. We painted the exterior warm gray, quite a shift from its traditional white. The interior also changed drastically; we paneled parts of the walls, and covered the rest with wallpaper. Mimi replaced the bulky TV set with a swanky 48-inch plasma TV. I bought a less intrusive, spanking-new B&O music system to dominate the mood in the living room. We gave the kitchen a more contemporary look, almost like a stage set where cooking wasn't a daily chore, but rather an option to indulge ourselves in great master chef styles.

When the house was finally ready to move in, I used my handsome work bonus to buy a brand-new car for Mimi; she had always admired the sleek look of the Mercedes CLK convertible. We had everything we wanted; at least, it had looked that way.

I pressed the buzzer at the main gate and started walking down the driveway. Lisa spotted me from upstairs and came running. "Daddy, Daddy, you're really here!" She hugged me and dragged me in. "Come, I wanna show you my birthday dress."

I saw Doreen, our housekeeper, standing by the door. We greeted each other as Lisa started pulling me with all her strength. The warm touch of her tiny hands filled my heart.

That being a Saturday, I expected both Lisa and Matthew to be at home. But Lisa told me that Matthew had started taking math tuitions on Saturdays. "Mom will pick him up on her way back," she explained.

We spent the whole afternoon playing games and in idle chitchat.

Suddenly the doorbell rang, and Lisa screamed, "Dad, Mom is here."

My heart started beating faster, and the hot and humid Singapore weather wasn't helping at all. I was perspiring. Yes, I wanted to see them all; but when Mimi was at the doorstep, it all seemed too complicated. Should I shake hands with her or hug her like good friends? For a moment, I wanted to run, but I knew that wasn't an option. Both Lisa and I opened the door. Matthew hugged me and said, "Dad, I missed you."

"I missed you too, son. What's new in school? Any girlfriend yet?"

"Eew, Dad!" Matthew ran upstairs to change.

I looked at Mimi; she smiled and said, "How was your Europe trip?"

"Great, indeed. I loved it."

"Tell us all about it. Do you want coffee?"

"Sure." I felt so relieved; turned out that I was stressed out for nothing.

Lisa's birthday party that evening was great—like a carnival in our living room. By five o'clock the whole living room swarmed with Lisa's friends, screaming and shouting, running after each other, and dragging the beautifully decorated streamers and balloons down to the floor and kicking them around everywhere. It was fun in complete chaos.

Mimi moved the dinner table to one corner, and the kids rushed over as soon as the food was served. But suddenly everything came to a pin-drop silence as Doreen wheeled in a huge birthday cake, beautifully decorated with pink-and-white icing. Mimi had planned everything in great detail, right down to a magic show that kept Lisa and her friends glued to the tricks. I sat there the whole time thinking, indeed, wouldn't it be nice if we could make all the unpleasant parts of our life vanish by a cool magic trick? On the other hand, would everything really be okay if we could wipe out a couple of bad days from our lives? After all, Mimi and I'd had a few great years together. Of course, it would've been so much easier on the kids. But I didn't think either of us wanted that.

After a while, Mimi came and sat next to me. "Thank you for coming back for her birthday. I know you weren't due back so soon. But you made Lisa very happy."

I would've loved to make Mimi happy, too; but I knew that was beyond me. I just said, "I'm happy to be here. You've done a great job in planning the party."

I was glad that there was nothing awkward between us; and I was relieved to have crossed the first hurdle in our new relationship as ex-partners.

But my time with Mr. Barco and Kevin had opened my eyes, and they had also taught me that I couldn't live in the past; I needed to move on with my life. After coming back to my apartment that night, I promised myself that I wouldn't make the same mistake ever again; I couldn't let Adeline slip away due to any non-communication leading up to any misunderstanding between the two of us. I must share my thoughts with her. I hadn't forgotten what Mr. Barco had told me about letting my partner into my world. No more romanticizing and solitary trips in my mind; I wanted to tell her everything that had been happening inside my head. I wanted to tell her how much I had been missing her.

I decided to write an email and explain everything, but before I could do anything, an email from her popped up as soon as I opened my laptop. Suddenly my heart started thumping and my palms got all sweaty; I was dumbstruck. I sat there motionless, unable to click open that message. From the subject header I couldn't figure out what it was about; it read, "Hi! How're you doing?" But did she really want to know how I was doing, or was there more to it?

Now that I was all alone in my own apartment, everything was coming back to me like a gigantic wave. Of course, we'd had a great time in Vienna. With Adeline, every minute of life was living; there wasn't a dull moment. One day, as we were walking along the Kärntner Strasse near the Opera House, she had suddenly disappeared from my side. As I started looking for her and walked back a few paces, she waved from a roadside café. I rushed back and asked, "What happened?"

"Nothing. Just wanted to see how long it takes before you notice that."

"Notice what?"

She didn't answer me. Instead, she lifted her right hand above her head and pointed her forefinger at herself, and shrugged.

"Of course, I would know if you suddenly disappeared from my side." I pulled out a chair at the opposite side of the table.

She giggled. "The question wasn't if, it was when you would notice my disappearance."

Almost a month later, that laughter suddenly echoed in my Singapore apartment. It took me more than fifteen minutes before I could sit down to look at my laptop again. I was trying to find any excuse to avoid opening that message. I paced up and down, poured myself a drink, and finally sat down, closed my eyes, and clicked. It was a brief email:

Hey, where are you? Haven't seen you online for a while. Are you lost or hiding, knowing well that you can't hide forever?

I thought we had shared a special relationship. Maybe that's just me. However, if you don't feel the same way anymore, we definitely need closure so we both can move forward.

Love you, Ade

Who would've ever believed that came from a twenty-three-year-old girl? Yes, Ade was right; I couldn't hide forever. I decided to write back. But what could I possibly say? Sorry? Or, that I liked her, but I couldn't commit to another relationship? That I was caught off guard? None of that made much sense. I had behaved like a coward. But I was no coward, was I?

Honestly, I wasn't so sure about love anymore. If I truly liked her, and I thought I did, then why hadn't I said anything to her? I knew it was complicated; I was carrying a lot of baggage and I panicked. I had feared my relationship with Ade might throw Lisa and Matthew to second position in my mind; definitely I wasn't ready for that. How could I explain such a delicate problem to her?

But I decided to apologize for my behavior. If needed, I would go back to Vienna to offer peace. The problems were solely mine, and I would deal with those myself. Maybe I needed more time. But why should she suffer for no fault of hers? I immediately sent a reply, and felt relieved, as though a weight had been lifted off my chest.

But that only took care of the first half of the problem; the other half would be waiting for an answer. I looked at the time: 10:35 p.m. That would be 5:35 p.m. in Vienna; Ade should be back from her class soon, unless she had gone grocery shopping before coming back home. I decided to wait. Again, I paced the apartment a couple of times. I poured myself another glass of water. I looked at my watch; it was 10:47 p.m. Unbelievable! When did my watch stop? I ran to my computer; it also showed 10:47 p.m. I couldn't believe that it had been only twelve minutes. It seemed like an hour to me. It was funny; a few days before, I had avoided every chance of coming in contact with her again, but after sending that email I couldn't wait another minute to hear what she had to say.

I went to the balcony for fresh air. Singapore at night looked gorgeous from the twenty-third floor. It had rained a little earlier that evening, and everything emerged squeaky clean. This part of Singapore had gone through major redevelopment; they laid tiles on sidewalks and changed the old streetlights to Victorian-style lampposts.

Initially, we all had thought that was a rather odd choice; why put carved period light fittings in a modern city like Singapore? But now, from a distance, I appreciated the way they looked—elegant and exquisite. I was particularly glad because it reminded me of the old city of Vienna and my time with Adeline there. Suddenly I couldn't stop thinking about her. Everything gushed out forcibly like water as if someone has pulled the drain stopper in a bathtub after a nice, long bath; everything I had held back wanted to get out of my control, all at the same time.

She had told me, "Each life is like another book at the library; there're thousands in there. It's your choice whether you want your readers to find you in adventure, comedy, or romance, or in the thriller section. It depends on how you build and live your life; it revolves around your likes and dislikes. We have a duty to our readers. Nobody likes a half-told story; nobody wants to read half a book. It must be complete, or nothing. The bestsellers are always stories well told—candid, effortless, unpretentious, and uninhibited. I want people to find me in the romance category. But I don't want just anyone to read me; I would prefer to go home with only those who're serious about romance. So, what kind of book do you want to be, Rohan?"

Frankly, I had no idea where I belonged. Yes, I had been romantic once; but I wasn't sure about love now. Those who can truly love, they're like candles; they don't mind sacrificing themselves for the sake of love. But the rest of us are candleholders. We love and appreciate the light of love, but are too afraid to burn ourselves down to light up someone else's life.

The sound of an email alert brought me back to real time. Yes, Ade must've come back home, and had already replied:

Hey! Glad you're still alive. You had me worried. Gotta go back to my part-time job in three hours. Must go to sleep now. Will catch up over the weekend.

Love you. Ade

Amazing girl! She acted as if nothing had happened. I had feared she would be fuming, but she seemed fine. She didn't even want to know where I had been or what I had been doing; she didn't ask anything.

It's true that we all love to live without confrontation, but we get tangled up in the web of practical living. Ade was above all that. She hadn't asked me anything that anyone else would've thought questionable. Was she a saint or what? The more I came to know that girl, the deeper I sank.

Chapter 12

WHILE STAYING with Mr. Barco in Lauterbrunnen, I had promised myself that I wouldn't take my mother's love for granted anymore, and I would do everything in my power to bring back the smile on her face. So, without wasting any time, I went to see my mother the morning after Lisa's party. As much as I wanted her to stay in Singapore, after what Mr. Barco had told me, I knew I couldn't ignore her wishes anymore. I decided to go along with her decision to return to our family home in Goa. Fortunately, at my mother's insistence, my dad had kept that small family house in India.

After leaving it unattended for many years, he had hired a caretaker a few years back to look after the house. Now that my dad was gone, my mother had no reason to live in Singapore. This time, without any argument, I told her that I would dedicate my next few days to make that happen. I wanted to bring Matthew and Lisa, too, and make a family holiday out of it, but their school schedule didn't permit it.

The renovation in Goa turned out to be more work than I had anticipated. The caretaker had done the best he could. We decided to stay in a nearby hotel to expedite the process. The close proximity to the house made the supervision easier.

Once the basics were done, five weeks later, we moved in; and I helped my mother rearrange everything, piece by piece, to her liking. The smell of fresh paint, the delightfully finished wooden floors, and the panoramic view of the Arabian Sea brought the old dilapidated house to life again. My mother looked happy. I hadn't seen her smile like that since my dad was alive. I guess Mr. Barco was right; she had her reasons, whether I wanted to understand them or not.

Living in Goa for those few days brought back so many images from the past, images that I had thought were lost forever in a vast sea of memories. I took long walks along the beaches and sat there for hours, much like I used to do in my childhood days. Strong summer breeze sprayed seawater all over me, and the old memories—one after another—came crashing in waves.

My childhood days flashed before my eyes like yesterday. While other kids my age were busy playing soccer or beach volleyball, I had been perfectly at peace with my solitary thoughts. I would spend whole afternoons wandering aimlessly in the wilderness, searching for clues to the purpose of my existence.

Unfortunately, nineteen years later, I still didn't have my answers. Now, I know that even if I sat there the whole day, I wouldn't find anything. The nostalgia part was all good; but not being able to make much progress in my search made me little sad.

I decided to go for a drive to clear my head before I went back home. I drove for about ten—fifteen minutes on the open road with the Arabian Sea on my right. However, as soon as I got on the highway, the traffic came to a complete halt. I looked out the window; I couldn't see anything beyond the cars lined up in front of me. In the distance there were cars glued to the road in the opposite direction as well. An accident must've blocked the road ahead.

About an hour later, the road was cleared, and we finally started moving—but at a crawling speed. Only one lane was accessible on both sides, and everyone's attempt to get out of the jam first made the traffic more chaotic. A little patience and consideration for others would've made the transition much smoother.

Why do we human beings always make things so chaotic? Where are we rushing to? I remembered when I was a child, I was always fascinated with the long lines of crawling ants. They marched to and fro in strict military discipline as if they were on a mission. I would look in awe at how they never deviated from the path to their destination. Sometimes they moved in both directions, much like the traffic I was in; yet there would be no chaos or overtaking one another. The most amusing thing was when two ants crawling in opposite directions would suddenly stop to exchange pleasantries. I had no idea why they did that or what they said to each other, or if they were saying anything at all, but it reminded me of two friends accidentally meeting each other on a road trip and moving on after a few polite words.

But those days, my curiosity didn't stop there. I would often pick up an ant from that long line of crawling creatures and let it move slowly all over my hand as I watched it attentively. The ant would relentlessly look for an exit—crawling over and over at the same place, but it never stopped; it never gave up. After playing with it for a while, when my hand started to ache I would drop the ant at the same spot I picked it up from, and the ant would soon crawl back to join the others. It made me feel powerful, fooling that ant into thinking that it had traveled long and far, whereas in actual fact it hadn't gone anywhere. At the same time, it made me weak in the knees to wonder, what if someone unknown was playing the same game with me.

Indeed, decades later, I was back in the same place, much like those ants. I was still searching for answers to the same questions. The only difference was that the game had intensified over the years. And I couldn't afford not to get my answers this time.

One day, in the spirit of excavating the past, I decided to walk to my old school. I stood in front of the building and looked at the old, run-down structure in awe for several minutes, as if it'd been preserved by the World Heritage Committee. Indeed, the school building had preserved the memories of thousands of students like me; it had inscriptions on every wall, telling the success stories and the sad stories as well.

My school days weren't such happy days. I always had too many questions, and my teachers would say, "Those aren't important; concentrate on your class notes now." I didn't like that; my dad always told me that I had a right to ask why. He would say that if I asked why and how, I wouldn't have to memorize everything. Although I found that advice very helpful later in my life, unfortunately it didn't pay immediate dividends during my school days.

As a result, I hated going to school. My grades kept falling, and I barely passed each year and made it to the next class. My sister was quite the opposite; she was a brilliant student and every teacher loved her, which made matters worse at home. My mother always complained, "Why can't you be more like your sister, Rita?"

Of course, it would've been much easier for me too, if I were more like my sister. But I always found our textbooks stale and disconnected from our life. I needed a logical connection to put things in perspective. I wanted to know how far I was from the Amazon rainforest before I could answer any questions on the impact of their deforestation on global warming. Neither my textbooks nor my teachers had that covered. And I didn't want to memorize stuff I didn't understand or couldn't put in context.

The sudden sound of the school bell brought me back to my senses. I looked up from outside the building and saw students running around everywhere. I noticed the rather empty long hallway on the first floor next to the admin office. And I was struck by another flashback. Is there really such a thing as a sign from god? I don't think anybody knows for sure. However, if there was such a thing, then I definitely got a glimpse of it on June 19, 1990. I would never forget that date. All signs that morning had promised a gloomy day. A tropical thunderstorm and heavy downpour had brought an end to an exceptionally humid summer that year in Goa; and as the day progressed, everyone was looking for shelter. Tides were high and the beaches were deserted. The ghastly winds made umbrellas useless, and the deadly lightning followed by loud thunder every now and then sent everyone packing. The roads were empty; the shops were shut. The only creatures on the streets were a few trembling dogs scavenging for food.

Most people decided to stay indoors and enjoy the relief brought by the monsoon, with the exception of those who were dreading the final year school results. It was impossible for me to wait until the rain stopped; it could take hours. I decided to brave the gods' fury, and when I reached my school, I found out that clearly I wasn't the only one.

Standing in the hallway that day, I felt my heart pounding louder than my stereo; my anticipation turned into apprehension, then into my worst nightmares. Suddenly it all flashed before my eyes: what had happened to some of the students who had failed to graduate before me. Filipe Antonio, the once-legendary high school heart-throb, had ended up running a dingy motel on Anjuna Beach; my two-year senior, the prom queen, and my elder sister's best friend, Zabel, got pregnant at seventeen and had ended up marrying Nikel, the greatest jerk on earth; "Big Pedru," the one-time soccer team captain, had settled for a bouncer's job across the street. They all had one thing in common: they'd had to give up their dreams to pay for their juvenile weaknesses. To think of it, all it took to derail their life was barely one mistake. I certainly didn't want to end up like them. Sure, my mistakes weren't quite like theirs; yet the end result could be the same. We all had one thing in common: we had avoided studying, and concerned ourselves with our personal whims.

An hour later that day, I had found out that I had bypassed a disaster. However, that couldn't make me happy. Compared to my sister's results two years before, I had scored really badly. With my results in hand, I decided that I would be anything in life but an average Joe. I was devastated not because I scored badly; I was sad because deep down in my heart, I knew I could've done better. That day I spent the next couple of hours sitting in the empty hallway, even after everyone else was long gone. I knew there would be repercussions. How would I ever build a future based on such lousy results? That helpless scene in the school hallway haunted me for a long time. I knew I had failed my father and my family; moreover, I had failed myself.

"Hello! You want to come inside?" A voice jolted me back from the past. I looked at the elderly gentleman; he seemed familiar. I must've seen him before. I remembered that well-built frame and the long hair, but his gray hair didn't quite fit in. As I delved deeper into my memory to search for that face, he came to my rescue.

"I'm the old caretaker, Shiva. Now I'm retired."

"How're you, Shiva?" I immediately remembered the strong, muscular man who always used to sit at the school gate. And by always, I really mean always—rain or shine, I had never seen our school gate unattended in my ten years there. "What're you doing here?" I asked.

"We still live here; my son works here now. Come, I'll show you your favorite tree."

He took me straight to the backyard behind the school buildings, plucked a couple of guavas from the fruit trees there, and handed them to me. I was speechless; I stood there with the guavas in my hand and my eyes wide open. He'd touched me someplace I thought was dead forever. Did he remember every incident and each student like that? During recess in our school days we often went there, sat on those low branches, and would sneak the fresh treats from the tree, until of course a few jealous kids told on us and Shiva would chase us away.

In fact, he didn't forget any of that. He even went on to apologize, "I'm sorry, Rohan; I was simply doing my job those days. I didn't have much choice. Now it's my son's job, and I don't see him anywhere near. So, take as many as you want." And he smiled.

"Don't worry about it, Shiva; I understand."

"Want to have a cup of tea, Rohan?"

"Maybe another day." I didn't want to keep my mother waiting; I quickly thanked Shiva and headed back to her house.

The timing for our Goa trip couldn't have been more perfect; Rita, my sister and her husband, Oliver, were attending a marine life conference in Dubai for three days, and they decided to drop by and visit us after the conference was over. They missed my father's funeral; and they were worried about my mother too. After all, Dubai was only a three-hour flight away.

Both Oliver and Rita were marine biologists, and they loved their work. They traveled the world, helping ravaged and ill-treated marine animals; they fought to pass animal rights bills and they spent all their time and money on a cause they believed was worth living and dying for. Once, when I had first joined my office, I also had felt that involved and connected to my work. There was a thrill and excitement in watching the market movements. At home, I would spend all my spare time watching the news or even the weather channels from all over the world. I knew that one political comment or one natural disaster could send the market into a tailspin almost immediately. But I didn't remember when and how all that passion had changed into making money. Good thing, Oliver and Rita never had changed their priorities.

They arrived in Goa on a Saturday morning. It had been so long since we had all seen one another. Even when my dad was alive, Oliver rarely visited our family. It wasn't because he didn't want to; it was because some helpless creatures somewhere on earth always needed him more. And Rita didn't want to come without him. Rita and I weren't the best of friends while growing up, but later on during my final years at school, I had realized that we had more things in common than we thought. We both loved nature, and our life philosophies were slowly moving in the same direction; we had also started sharing our books and our thoughts.

In the evening, Oliver and Rita came out to lay the dinner table on the balcony, and I gave them a hand. Our balcony took on a very different look that day; the wooden deck with its expansive view overlooking the sandy beach and the sea quickly turned into a beachside restaurant. Once we started getting the food from the kitchen, the dinner table seemed too small. In an over-enthusiastic cooking spree my mother had cooked so many dishes that we had no space on the table to put our plates. So, Oliver pulled another side table next to it.

In fact, while we were growing up, the dinner table in our house had never been big. It was always functional. We never had fancy dinners; hence, there was no expensive dinnerware. Our table was never laid with lines of unending cutlery. Yet my mother still taught us excellent table manners. During my childhood, I could never figure out why one needed so many forks and knives, or why there must be one set for fish and another for chicken. It didn't make any sense. My mother gave me an easy solution: "When you're served a fancy dinner with forks and knives lined up, start from the outside and work your way in. Tables are usually laid that way, so that it never leaves a hole in the middle." She used to say that was dinner rules for dummies. Suddenly remembering that incident, I almost laughed out loud until I realized I wasn't alone. But as soon as I reminded Rita about our childhood dinner lessons, she lost control and spilled our little secret. Everybody laughed.

With good food, a fruity and full-bodied Merlot, and great family company, the evening flowed like smooth jazz. Of course I missed Matthew and Lisa in this rare family reunion. But it was what it was; and I was slowly getting used to that idea.

After dinner Oliver and Rita went to the beach for a short walk. I couldn't help but admire them from the balcony. How come they always did everything right, and I did everything wrong? Indeed, they seemed exactly made for each other; they were always involved in each other's lives in more ways than one could possibly imagine. They had often filled in for each other at home and at many charity events, and they looked perfectly happy. Why couldn't we have done that in our marriage? Had they really found their connection to the eternal truth while I had been left clueless? Rita had always been a step ahead in academics during our childhood; but when I started working, I thought I was doing better than her professionally. Now I could see how stupid that was. While I focused on building a materialistic lifestyle, she created something meaningful: a relationship.

I was glad, at least, Oliver and Rita had found happiness in life. Honestly, I didn't know another couple who had as great a relationship as theirs. Could I get another shot at it with Adeline? But wouldn't that affect my search for finding a purpose in life? According to Mr. Barco, it shouldn't. The strong breeze and the roaring sounds of the waves in the growing dark echoed the same message. I didn't go to bed until quite late that night. I missed Adeline; she would've loved Goa.

Sometimes, we feel revived and refreshed in certain people's company; they make us feel good and surround us with vigorous vitality. I often wondered why. Was it the energy they exuded? Adeline's company was truly refreshing like that. It was much like what we experience at a beautiful sea beach, in a remote log cabin, or up in a hilltop bungalow. We feel extremely sad for the first few days after coming back from these places because they've one thing in common: they all have stimulating energy fields that slowly work within our body and mind, and we get used to that. And when we leave these places, we miss that energy around us and experience a vacuum, much like lack of oxygen. Imagine what would happen if we could pack a slice of that energy field in our luggage and bring it back with us? At least I wouldn't have been missing Adeline so much.

After Oliver and Rita left, it was my turn to leave Goa. It had taken me almost a month and a half to settle everything there, and as much as I wanted to see my mother happy, I was still very unsure about leaving her all alone; I didn't like the idea at all. But my mother was insistent. She told me that she wasn't prepared when my dad passed away, but she wanted to stand ready for her turn. "You see, Rohan," she said, "life on earth is temporary; death is only painful or sad if you aren't prepared for it."

"How can anyone be prepared for it, Mom?"

"Let me give you an example. If you go on a vacation for five days, you come back all rejuvenated. And you probably won't complain even once. But imagine it's a two-week getaway, and you receive a call on the sixth day asking you to go back to settle an important client's urgent requests. Now that might make you sad. The question is, why? It's not because you didn't have any fun; you already enjoyed yourself for five days. It's because your mind wasn't prepared to end it yet. It's all in our mental preparation—how we feed the mind—whether we see any situation as permanent or temporary. The mind only becomes upset when we've to cut short a two-week holiday to five days. The trick here is in keeping your mind ready for departure from this world after a certain age. That way, if you live a few extra years, you'll treat that as a gift or a bonus. I haven't heard anybody complaining about an extended vacation," and she smiled.

I took comfort in knowing my mother's perspective. But I was more intrigued by what she said about our life here being temporary. Did that mean we move on to a permanent place from here or to another temporary life? All in all, where is the end?

Chapter 13

I WANTED TO SEE Lisa and Matthew as soon as I touched down in Singapore; I really missed them. But of course with the change in our situation, I couldn't see them when I wished. In a divorce, one of the partners has to give up more than the other, otherwise you have to go through a nasty custody battle. Mimi and I didn't want to drag our kids into it; we didn't want to break them up. I thought sharing custody would've been a torture to them as well; living in two places and traveling up and down every week didn't seem like a good idea to me. Why should they pay for our mistakes? So, I decided to give up custody to allow minimal disruption to their daily lives. Sometimes love means sacrifice; and I decided to walk away, leaving behind half of my heart.

From the airport I went straight to my apartment, changed, and decided to stop by to see the children before I went out for a jog. Unfortunately, since it was a Saturday morning, Lisa had gone out with Mimi for her piano lessons. But Matthew was at home and said he wanted to join me on my run. I knew he wasn't much of a runner; I wasn't even sure whether he liked it. "Are you sure?"

He sounded confident. "Dad, wait up. I wanna go."

Taking the underpass at the Expressway we reached the East Coast Beach in fifteen minutes, and we continued running on the paved walking trail for another five minutes or so. By then Matthew was gasping for breath. We slowly walked up to his favorite big rock at the East Coast Park and sat down facing the sea, our feet dangling. It was quiet out there. The morning South China Sea was still under a lazy spell. Only a few calorie-conscious Singaporeans were trying to outdo each other in jogging, biking, or rollerblading. Fragments of white clouds passed overhead. The smell of seawater filled the air.

Matthew looked at me and said, "Hey, Dad, can I ask you something? When do you have to leave? I like it when you're here."

"I like it too, son; but I'm planning to go someplace else after I finish a couple of things here."

"But this is also your home, right?"

"It was; but now I have to find a new place. I'm thinking of going to Phuket for a while. That's a beautiful place, right? Don't you love the beaches there? And what about the seafood, huh?" I tried to divert his attention.

"Yeah, it's great, Dad. But does that mean Mom and you are never getting back together?" He insisted on getting an answer. Matthew was right; we all want clarity. We all want to know where we stand and where we're heading.

"I'm sorry, son."

We were both quiet for a while. I pulled him closer and held him tight. I could feel his pain and the void inside. I would've felt the same way if I'd had to grow up without my dad. It was like my mother used to say: our children are part of us, so when they're in pain, it hits us the same way.

I didn't know how to offer him relief; I was lost for words. Inadvertently, I blurted out something stupid to cover up my inadequacy. "You want ice cream?"

"I'm not four, Dad. I'm seven. And no thanks, I don't want ice cream in the morning."

"I'm sorry, son. I understand. But you know what, I learned a very valuable lesson in Europe: change is good, whether we like it or not. The faster we accept it, the easier life becomes. Look at yourself; you're changing too. Aren't you growing taller every day? Trust me, I know the feeling; I felt the same way too when my dad passed away."

Matthew was silent for a while. He looked away to the open sea and then suddenly asked, "Where did Grandpa go, Dad? What happens to a person after death?"

I immediately regretted not having that conversation earlier. We all had gone to my dad's funeral a couple of months before, but I had been so busy with my own problems that I had forgotten to have a talk with him about his grandfather's death. It was the children's first experience of death in the family; of course, his questions were only natural. How had I missed that? I immediately apologized.

"No worries, Dad. I'm just wondering."

"You're not the only one, son; to tell you frankly, people are still searching for an answer with a degree of certainty. Many people think only the body dies, but the soul or the spirit lives on. Some think we go to heaven after death. Others believe there's no birth or death of a spirit; once our body dies, the soul finds a place in another body, like in a newborn baby. In other words, it changes its shell, much like when we change houses if our existing habitat becomes unlivable. And they further believe that all these spirits are part of one greater spirit that has infinite power and is everywhere."

I went silent for a while. I was trying my best, but I wasn't so sure that I was doing a very good job at explaining death, or whether I had even made any sense at all.

Matthew didn't say another word other than, "Dad, I'm hungry. Can we go home now?"

"Sure, son."

When I went to bed that night I couldn't think of anything but my morning conversation with Matthew. Well, what is death? All we know for sure is that after death the body no longer exists in this mortal world. Few cremate it and many bury the dead, but either way the body merges with nature. In one sense, that's the end. But I had difficulty acknowledging that as the end of it all.

I knew there were people who could give a detailed description of their past life, so I couldn't ignore reincarnation. However, not many people can remember their past life; not everyone is reincarnated. But what does reincarnation mean to us? Probably nothing. But it surely does make us curious to know more. Some religions tell us that if we do good work in this life, we'll get a better life next time. Yet who can prove that? Who is able to see both their past and present life together, side by side, in order to compare which one is, indeed, better? Sadly, until then it'll always remain a theory; there'll be ambiguities.

That's where some religions bring in the soul or spirit. Still, the question remains, how can anyone understand the soul, much less translate it into words. Then again, maybe that's supposed to stay a mystery, like life itself.

We can make arguments and counterarguments, but we'll never know for sure whether there's life after death or what happens to us after death. Does it really matter? Whether a person believes in karma or life after death or heaven, the belief brings optimism to life; it provides one with the incentive to do good work in this life to prepare them better for the next life, if it exists. So, while life after death remains debatable, the belief itself gives hope to those born deprived, disabled, underprivileged, and troubled. They know that this is not the end of it all, and that they'll have their day in the sun; they'll laugh again, they'll be happy someday, and they'll have another shot at life to make it all different. And that, without judging right or wrong, is worth believing.

As I lay there my dad's face suddenly appeared in front of me. There was a glow around his face. I was able to see him in the darkness of the room, and he was smiling. I didn't feel sad anymore; he looked so peaceful. And soon, I fell into a deep sleep.

* * *

The next morning, when I woke up in my bed, I felt a heavy weight on my chest. I had an opportunity to rediscover myself during the recent Goa trip. Living close to so many childhood memories made me realize what I had been missing. But the reality in Singapore was very different; there was no room to accommodate a guy like that. He would be a total misfit. How had that happened? Something must've gone wrong somewhere along the way. I dragged myself to the balcony with a cup of coffee; I needed an answer. As I traveled back and forth between my childhood days in Goa and my married life in Singapore, those two lives looked like they belonged to two different people from two opposite poles.

As a child, I was always intrigued by each connectivity in the universe that played out in front of my eyes. I couldn't believe that the calm, serene, and the glowing moon I saw at night outside my window had anything to do with the rise and fall of the waves in the sea. How could the moon, from miles and miles away, be the cause of the high tides and the low tides? After all, I had seen the Arabian Sea swelling many times in front of my eyes from a gentle, calm demeanor to a ferocious one in a matter of hours.

As my dad explained things like gravity, which I could only fathom as a mystery at that age, I was quite convinced that each one of us was a part of that big play too. I knew the sun and the moon had their roles to play; even the plants and trees had work cut out for them. But what would be my role in the universe? What was I supposed to do? At school, the classes that didn't fit into my quest, but instead asked me to memorize things, became monotonous and unacceptable to me. I devoted all my time and energy to finding my role in the universe—and I kept ignoring my grades.

Then what changed everything? What made me forget my quest? Was it Singapore that made me such a materialistic guy? No, I couldn't say that. On the other hand, Singapore wasn't like anything I had ever imagined. I loved everything there from day one. I guess the poor score in my final school exam had shaken me really badly, and I saw a real opportunity to turn my life around in Singapore.

When I first came here, there was no time to waste in idle daydreaming on the beach; I had to concentrate more on my classes. But it was easy this time, because I loved my classes and my new teachers there, and I enjoyed what I was learning.

Maybe I had been a little odd all my childhood. But I was no saint, and I definitely couldn't sit by and do nothing when a girl like Mimi came into my life. What was I supposed to do? Walk away? But even now after all that had happened, I wasn't sorry that I didn't.

Mimi was smart and determined, and indeed, I had liked that about her. I had been shy all my life, and she was bold. I remembered how much I had to struggle before I could comfortably embrace any change or new people in my life. It took me years to gather up the courage to go see her parents with her; 'Is that really necessary?' was my usual excuse. Whereas, she was quite the opposite; she jumped up in excitement when I first told her about my mother's invitation for dinner on a weekend.

The truth is, I knew she was out of my league. And that made it all the more challenging. Since our family had moved to Singapore, I had faced many new challenges; but getting Mimi to like me was another kind of challenge entirely. I did everything in my power to impress her. I had never been hypnotized in my life; but I bet it would surely feel something like getting to know Mimi. Spending every minute with her was like living a fantasy. I didn't know what I was doing. I felt intoxicated in her presence, and I craved more.

Everything happened at lightning speed. I had never imagined that I would hit a home run so soon on only our second date. That day, after I had parked the car by her front porch, we slowly walked to the entrance; she unlocked the thick wooden door and pushed it open. She might have used a bit more force than was actually needed. But she couldn't have been drunk, because each of us had only two glasses of wine. Then she stepped inside and looked back; I leaned forward to kiss her goodnight, but when I looked directly into her eyes, they resembled a vast ocean whose depth would be anybody's guess. Her gaze pierced my heart as if it was searching for an answer. I don't know what she found there; but she suddenly grabbed me by my front collar, pulled me inside with a jolt, and closed the door behind us. And that door didn't open for the next forty-eight hours.

Three years later, the obvious followed: the invitations, the pre-wedding jitters, and the wedding bells. It was a big ceremony, not because we wanted it that way; in fact, we had hoped for a small, quiet family affair. But before we knew it, Mimi's parents hijacked the event; and their intervention blew everything out of proportion. They soon established a clear chain of command. Obviously, Mrs. Tan was the boss. Mimi and I were practically guests at our own wedding. But that didn't bother us much; we didn't care to get involved in all the wedding planning, anyway. Our idea of a small get-together to celebrate the event finally turned out to be a much, much bigger party.

However, the party didn't last long for us. But that couldn't be the reason for my moral slide. It wasn't Singapore, and it wasn't Mimi; I had only myself to blame. But where exactly did I lose myself? Loving someone couldn't be wrong. But did I love Mimi for all the wrong reasons? Superficial elements are hard to cling to. Was it wrong to have a higher ambition? I guess Mr. Barco was right: ambition is good as long as it doesn't hurt others. But mine did; and to think of it, my ambition was all self-serving.

I loved the lifestyle that Singapore and Mimi represented; but it took time before I comprehended that there was more to life than material success. There would always be one podium higher than the present one, and another yet higher than that.

An ambulance screeched through the roads outside. I looked out at the Singapore landscape. It had changed a lot since we first came here in the early nineties, though it still looked as pretty from the twenty-third-floor balcony. That was a Sunday; so there wasn't much traffic on the road. I could see the South China Sea on the eastern horizon, still covered in mist.

Chapter 14

THE EUROPE TRIP had helped me get clarity on a couple of my problems. I was finally at peace with my mother's relocation; the happiness I saw in her face in Goa told me that I had done the right thing. I would possibly miss my kids all my life; that would be a lifetime work in progress, but I felt better seeing them adjusting well to the changes in our family.

Now it was time to get my own life back on track. I had been pretending to be on top of the world for a long time, while in actual fact I had been leading a blindfolded life. The continuous conflict and chaos inside my head had made me restless. As much as I wanted to stand out in life; I now realized that this had nothing to do with having a better job title or earning more money. I was finally done with the corporate rat race. I made up my mind and decided to quit.

A moral dilemma had been eating me up for the last few years. Initially, I had loved my work because it came with both challenges and rewards. But recently it had come to a point where the key performance indicator had shifted drastically; the better a person was at lying and deception, the higher the rewards would be. I loved intellectual challenges, but this emotional challenge was too much. I was definitely not that person, at least not anymore. Once the blindfold of insecurity came off, I knew what to do. I couldn't keep recommending stocks just to help my company earn more in brokerage fees, exposing my clients to vulnerability. My clients trusted me with their millions, so, the least I could do was be truthful to them. It was time to move on.

Mr. Barco's words had helped me decide a course of action. The way to my final destination still looked murky, but I knew I had to stay the course, no matter what. First, I must regain my peace of mind. Most certainly, I couldn't do anything if I had to constantly justify my actions to myself. I knew changing a profession at thirty-six wouldn't be an easy task. However, I felt glad that for the first time in a long while, I thought I knew the way forward. I had no idea what I would be doing next; but I was pretty sure of what I didn't want to do anymore. To me that was definitely a step in the right direction.

But unsure as I was, I still had to look for another livelihood. I could follow my dad's footsteps and take up teaching; Singapore always had a shortage of teachers. But long before I became a stock market analyst and a portfolio manager, there was a time I had wanted to become a writer. In between, whenever I glanced through any of my old files, I missed writing. But those days if the idea of being a full-time writer ever crossed my mind, I had always ignored it. Maybe I was too scared to make financial sacrifices. In recent years, all I had written were technical reports on market issues, but in my school and college days I wrote short stories and often got them published. Well, I thought, I could give it a fresh try. To think of it, once I left my office, I would've plenty of time to write.

So, this might be the opportunity to take my next big step: fiction. Writing wasn't totally new to me, but to make it a profession would definitely be a challenge. And I guess the thought of a challenge was all that was necessary to get me started again. I remembered what Mr. Barco had told me one day: "Each and every human being is a walking double-A battery. Their real power is never manifested unless being tested."

Now when I thought about it again, I recognized how true it could be. Without batteries, our beloved iPhones and iPads are as good as dead. They come alive as soon as we put in new batteries or recharge them; and these gadgets immediately show what they are capable of. Similarly, maybe my writing could also recharge my life again.

I was sure I couldn't sit by the sidelines anymore, like double-A batteries sit on supermarket shelves. I needed to act fast. The following months would be a trying time for me, but I was all set. Become a writer? An ambitious goal, indeed, for an ex–portfolio manager, as many would say. But I was ready to take up that challenge.

After making the decision, I felt much lighter at heart and even happy. I knew there wouldn't be a regular paycheck for a long period of time. But I didn't mind, and I was ready to work for it again. Besides, my savings and investments could take care of a moderate lifestyle for a while, and that was all I really needed.

Although I had a long road ahead, my vision became clearer. And having decided on my future path, I had only one thing left to do. The following week, I rejoined my office after three months' leave and handed in my resignation. My bosses had always loved me, so they told me the same thing they had told me before: "Break-up is hard; but everything will be okay with time." But I knew it wouldn't be. Because, I didn't want them to be okay anymore; I was done with my superficial marriage and my phony success. I had moved on. I had a new goal in sight.

The next morning, to everyone's surprise, I left my corner office for good to pursue my goals in writing. At my request, my bosses didn't break the news to my colleagues; I had decided to tell them myself. They all wished me good luck and success in my writing. For sure, few of them probably thought it was weird; but none said anything. A number of them even sought my advice on their future career paths.

The whole morning, I noticed the absence of one person: Tina. Later I found her sitting all alone in her cubicle without even looking at what was going on in my office. I walked up to her and said, "Hi!" She was caught totally unprepared. She didn't look up; I thought I saw teardrops on her desk, and her wastebasket was filled with tissues. She wanted to speak, but her voice failed her; she quietly raised her left hand with her forefinger open, indicating she needed a minute.

I knew what that meant. I said, "I'll wait for you in my office," and left her alone.

Tina showed up within five minutes. I didn't want to say good-bye to Tina abruptly like the way I did to other colleagues. Whether I wanted to admit it or not in the past, now I knew that I couldn't be insensitive to her feelings. I must do it like a gentleman. "Tina, let's go grab lunch later this week. I've stuff to discuss with you. How about Friday?"

Her eyes suddenly glittered; she said, "I'd love to. . . but can we do Saturday dinner instead? Lunch is always such a rush here; I hate to go out."

I had nothing much going on; Saturday was fine with me too. But I was little worried about what her husband, Thomas would make out of it. Tina said, "He's out of town, and wouldn't be back until the following week," and she had nothing else to do.

* * *

I had never met Tina for dinner like that. It had always been business. However, she had always maintained that it was never just business between the two of us. That Saturday evening, she was the first to break the ice. "Hey, how is your book coming along? You want to read it to me one day?"

"Where did you hear that?" I was quite surprised.

"The little birds you're talking to the other day, they're chirping something like that." She smiled.

"I haven't started anything yet; just been thinking."

"Come on, it's me. I know you; you wouldn't have said anything unless you'd been halfway through, right?"

"You're right; that would've been the old me—too afraid to fail. Honestly, I still have no clue what I'm going to write about."

Tina looked little bewildered, but she sounded confident. "Don't worry; you'll figure it out. You always do."

I actually liked that. For a minute, I thought she could be a friend. That vote of confidence was like any true friend would've given, sticking by your side without judging you.

Before going out that evening, I had thought that after an early dinner, I would head back home. But Tina being Tina, didn't want to let go of a precious weekend evening so quickly. She said, "The night is young, and it's Saturday. Let's go for a drink."

When we finally ended up in a crowded pub on Boat Quay, the music was so loud that we could hardly hear one another. After we strained our voices for nearly twenty minutes, she bent close to my ear and said, "Don't gloat; but you're right. Let's go sit outside."

We found ourselves a table right next to the river. The Singapore River in front was quiet but charming, and the music didn't sound so bad from there. We sat in silence for a while. Tina had changed a lot. Maybe we grow up fast once we are in a relationship; and the bad ones make us grow up faster. Nothing wears us down more than a stressful relationship. Tina's face couldn't hide that even under her immaculate makeup.

After a couple of vodka tonics, Tina opened up as quickly as a water lily in a pond. She told me everything: how she had met Thomas—her two-year senior schoolmate. Thomas went to college in Sydney, and had been working there ever since. She narrated in detail how she met him again at a conference in Singapore, and how he had proposed to her barely after two months of dating. "Everything happened so fast that I lost track. The fact that we had known each other for a long time helped; Thomas said he'd get a transfer and proposed. I said yes. Did I make a mistake? I guess I was too scared to end up alone. ...Anyway, here I am, married for almost two years. How about that?"

"You did nothing wrong; you took a chance on love. That's what we human beings do."

We both kept quiet for a while. Is this relationship thing tough on everyone? Sooner or later, why do we all end up regretting our decisions? I looked around us. There was nothing much happening on the riverfront. Only a few tourist boats, once in a while, disrupted the reflection of the tall buildings on the otherwise calm water.

Tina took another sip from her glass and continued, "He's a great guy. He always has been. But I still feel there's a vacuum." Her fidgety movements and shifting eyes told me that there was more underneath all that, but she didn't elaborate any further; and I didn't want to ask. "You know what," she said, "Marriage is a complex institution. It's difficult to get in, and it's even more difficult to get out."

I didn't know how to respond to that. I was no expert in marriage either. My view toward the whole institution had also changed in the last few years. I stopped swirling the wine in my glass and then leaned back against the chair. "You know something? Marriage is like a sailboat. It's pretty when you see it from the shore. It sails nicely with a little wind; and if the wind is in your favor, you'll possibly reach your destination without doing a damn thing. However, the moment you try to steer it in the opposite direction of the wind, it's goddamn hard. Similarly, in a marriage if you go with the flow—with the other person's wishes and aspirations—it'll be a smooth sail; the moment you want to go against it, your marriage becomes as hard as sailing against the wind."

Tina looked confused. "Aren't husband and wife supposed to work as a team?"

Conventionally, Tina was right; but my experience had taught me otherwise. Most people enter into a marriage without knowing what that actually means; once into it, they find out that each person is on their own, and it's a much more difficult balancing act than maneuvering a sailboat. It's a constant juggling of words and actions. One cannot lie; so one tends to omit, or use words that can go either way. No one wants to look extravagant; so they hide from each other the things they buy. When they don't want to attend an event with their partner, they falsely bury themselves under work, house chores, or even under their children's school activities.

Tina was still waiting for my answer. Finding me lost in my thoughts, she tapped her fork against her glass. "Hello! Where have you been?"

I felt a little embarrassed, and told her briefly what I had been thinking about. Then, I looked at the tiny ripples on the water; suddenly, the wind picked up from a gentle breeze all evening. The strong wind blew a few strands of hair over Tina's face. She flipped her head to push them back, and said, "Well, dating is one thing; but marriage or living together is quite another, because you're constantly trying to keep up with the image the other person likes. When you're dating you always wear your best clothes and best perfume, and even put on your best smile. The problem starts the moment you say, 'I do.' You begin to take each other for granted. Everyone knows that the naked self is going to come out eventually. It's not a matter of if; it's a matter of when."

I couldn't agree more. "One must also notice how quickly the attitude and the level of tolerance changes. The same person who always liked your fancy shoes and never failed to compliment you, after marriage—when the credit card bill arrives—might say, 'Was this new pair really necessary?' A girlfriend who always admired and appreciated your chivalrous qualities, like opening a door for another woman and holding it until she passed through, that same person as your wife might say, 'Damn it, she is nearly thirty and perfectly healthy; she can open her own door. Can you hurry?'"

We both laughed. I didn't know where the marriage bashing came from. Just another modern-day problem? Maybe. Then I looked at her and said, "Unlike with any physical injury, it's better to scratch this kind of hurt when the wound is still fresh. Otherwise, it might leave a permanent scar." I didn't want that happening to Tina or to anybody, for that matter. I continued, "I wonder why on earth we haven't imposed a compulsory marriage renewal. You can't continue doing business anywhere in the world unless you renew your business license every year. You have to renew your driver's license too. So, why do we make an exception when it comes to a marriage license? Why give the stamp of permanence to a difficult and fragile relationship? Are we afraid that given a choice, most people might not renew it?"

Tina liked the idea; she repeated, "Renewing a marriage license, huh? Mine will be up for renewal in two months." She smiled, and her big brown eyes sparkled.

I was glad the somber mood of the evening was finally over, and Tina was back to her old self; she was having fun. But I could see the marriage thing had shaken her badly.

I looked at my watch; it was already a quarter after one. We hadn't noticed how quickly time had passed. Talking to her had always been easy and effortless, but this meeting was also very different: this was the first time I had met her as a friend.

Tina seemed quite buzzed; but my quick glance at my watch didn't escape her eyes. She asked, "What's the hurry? You have to go someplace? …I'm free; I've no place to go to. How about one more round?"

I didn't know what to say. "I thought you were. . ."

"I was what. . . drunk? I'm having a good time, Rohan. Is that really such a crime?"

I apologized and quickly ordered another round.

When I finally dropped her off at home, I realized that she had moved back to her old apartment. But why? Why was she still holding on to that place? Was it just typical Singaporean's chronic property craze or she still felt insecure about her relationship with Thomas? I was too afraid to ask anything.

She went straight to her balcony and said, "Come on in for a minute, Rohan; I have something important to tell you."

"What's that?"

She asked me to close the door and get her a bottle of water from the fridge. I was a little shocked at first when I saw her in the balcony; she was sitting still in the darkness like a lousy pencil portrait on a wall—lifeless. Then she said, "Thomas is cheating on me."

I was definitely not ready for this. I quickly gathered myself and said, "Are you sure?" Unthinkingly, I pulled another chair close to her.

"I'm positive."

I told her how Mimi had misunderstood the whole thing between her and me, and how she blew it out of proportion. Tina interrupted and said, "She wasn't totally wrong. Now I know I shouldn't have posted those comments online. I'm sorry, Rohan."

"Don't worry about it; that's water under the bridge."

Suddenly she lost control and started crying. She had proof of the cheating; in fact, she had already spoken with the other woman. I pulled my chair closer and hugged her. She kept saying, "I'm so lost. What can I do, Rohan?" Tears rolled down her cheeks; I felt them on my shoulder too.

I didn't know what to say. I had never felt so useless in my life. But before I knew it, I felt her tongue inside my mouth. I quickly broke away from her.

"Whoa! Whoa! Whoa! What're we doing? We can't do this, Tina; that would be so wrong. Besides, you also don't want this. Now you are vulnerable. So, let's leave it there."

"But why, Rohan? What's so wrong about it? Are you seeing anyone?"

"Well. . . sort of."

"What's that supposed to mean?"

"I'm working on it."

I knew I had to tell her about Adeline; otherwise, it would get even more complicated than it already was.

After I finished, she quickly apologized and said, "Good luck, Rohan. I'm sorry if I put you in an awkward situation. Just so you know, I really like you. Don't you get it?"

I certainly didn't want to get into that conversation. I quickly looked at my watch and said, "Wow! It's a quarter after three in the morning. I gotta go now."

As she waved from the balcony, I pulled the door behind me. Once out in the open, I took a deep breath and thanked god for knocking some sense into me this time.

Chapter 15

MR. BARCO ONCE TOLD ME that while sleeping, our brain processes information and helps us solve many major problems. The next morning, I woke up with a decision I thought was my best option in many ways: I wanted to get away from Singapore, at least for some time, and live someplace else to figure everything out. During our separation, Mimi and I had decided that it would be wise to let her keep the Singapore house; that way the kids wouldn't be uprooted from their familiar environment. A couple of years before, we had bought a penthouse in Phuket for investment purposes; so I would keep that one. Phuket is a beautiful island in Thailand, only about a one-hour-forty-minute flight away from Singapore. We had been there a few times on short family holidays. Now moving to Phuket seemed like a great idea.

I knew I would be cut off from the world I had lived in for the last nineteen years, but that might be the best thing for everyone's sake. As it is, I couldn't live with Mimi and my kids in the same city and not be able to see them every day. That would be too painful. I couldn't act like nothing had happened, and move on with my life like business as usual. Not having a dog when you're a little kid is one thing, and then losing him for your own fault is quite another.

Besides, Phuket reminded me of my childhood days in Goa. I also thought the silence and the isolation might be good for my writing.

But before I left for Phuket, I wanted to take Matthew and Lisa out for a picnic, like we used to do before. Mimi had no reason to say 'no' to my plan; so I went to pick them up a little after five one evening that week. As Lisa and Matthew came running to the car, I smiled; I had a little surprise planned, too.

Lisa peeked in the car and jumped back. "Why do you've so many birds in there, Dad?"

"You'll see. First, buckle up."

Then she suddenly asked me a question I wasn't prepared for. "Why isn't Mom coming? Don't you want to ask her, Dad?"

I immediately realized I had made a big mistake. As quickly as we adults separate ourselves legally and emotionally, children may have more difficulty accepting those changes. Probably most children have seen their parents arguing or fighting over many family matters. Their little minds initially think the separation is like another fight; everything will be fine in few days. And when those days become weeks and months, they tend to worry. I should've been more sensitive. I looked at Lisa and said, "Yes, I do. But I wasn't sure whether she had anything going on. You guys wait here; I'll go ask her." And I jumped out of the car.

If Lisa and Matthew wanted her there, I must oblige them regardless of my feelings. But as I reached the front door, I stood there for a minute. I felt a little embarrassed for not asking her along. After all, we had vowed to remain friends. Or was I still harboring bad feelings toward her? If so, I had to nip it right away; we must move on as a family.

She answered the door. "You guys are still here? Forgot anything?"

"Yes…you."

Mimi smiled and said, "I didn't know you wanted me to come. I thought you wanted the kids to yourself for the evening."

"Not really. It wouldn't be the same without you."

However, Mimi didn't move or answer. Before, I would've felt insulted and walked out—not knowing that walking out at that stage would only worsen the situation. But now I knew better; possibly she felt hurt for not being asked earlier. I said, "I'm sorry; it was my mistake. I should've been more specific."

'Sorry' is, indeed, one of the most difficult and most powerful words in the English language, provided one can feel and say it at the same time. It's difficult because you sincerely need to feel the pain of the other person and rise above your ego to say it; it's powerful because you overwhelm the other with the opposite reaction of what they were expecting. Imagine the feeling of getting a hug from one instead of the slap you had been dreading. It's bound to move you.

I got my reward instantly. She said, "That's all right, Rohan. Let's not make a big deal out of it. Give me five minutes."

"Take your time."

As we drove off, everybody seemed curious about those birds again. Lisa said, "I don't like them in a cage, Dad."

"Me neither."

"Then why are you keeping them here?"

"You'll see."

We soon reached our favorite family picnic spot: Changi Beach. The kids loved that beach, but what they loved most was its proximity to the airport; every now and then, they could feel an oncoming airplane almost brushing their hair as it came in to land. Once we arrived, they immediately lay down on the slanted grass patch facing the sea and started screaming at the top of their voices every time a plane came over them.

Changi Beach had always worked like a magical time machine for me. The gusty wind, the seawater smell and the swinging palm trees instantly transported me back twelve years before, to when Mimi and I had our first picnic there. That evening had meant a lot to us. People say our true colors emerge in the face of real adversities. That day, for the first time, we saw each other close to any real danger.

The exact spot was closer to the next parking lot—and was about two hundred yards away from there into the sea. That place was, indeed, a sweet reminder of the old, rustic Changi Beach, before the roads were paved and tons of concrete were laid to build the promenade here. Twelve years before the place looked very different.

Mimi and I were also different: much younger, and two people in love. That day Mimi had prepared a picnic basket that could feed a whole village. She had everything from potato salad and mini chicken sandwiches to sausage rolls and pecan pie brownies. However, in all fairness to her, she was only twenty-two then; how would she know what to pack in a picnic basket for two?

I remembered that night in minute detail. The sky looked gorgeous with a zillion stars overhead. The gentle waves were beating on the shore. The strong wind heightened the ruffling of the palm and the coconut leaves as they danced vigorously in joy. There wasn't a creature in sight, and not a soul to disturb us; it was much like we owned the place.

The feeling that night was incredible; possibly nowhere else on earth one could feel so secluded and yet so protected. Just as I was admiring the safety and security in Singapore, I heard whispers around us, though I couldn't pinpoint which direction they came from. I asked Mimi, "Did you hear that?"

She shrugged. "Hear what?"

"People whispering?"

"Nope. You must've been dreaming."

I didn't want to argue; I wasn't quite sure, anyway. I quickly lay down next to her, watching the night sky. But after five minutes or so, I heard them again. This time the voices were clearer. They were speaking Chinese. I poked Mimi and asked, "Do you hear them now?"

"Shh! I can't make out what they're saying. They're speaking Hokkien."

"So? That's also Chinese, right?" I whispered.

"Don't you know we Singaporeans speak Mandarin? There're many other dialects; Hokkien is one of those. Can you stop bugging me and let me see whether I can make out anything."

"Okay, okay." I wanted her to concentrate, so I kept quiet.

We both sat there silently for the next few minutes. A while later we heard the voices again, coming from our left; I also heard the sound of people treading through the water.

From in between the leafy bushes, nothing was visible at first, even under the moonlight. After a couple of minutes I spotted a man walking toward us, holding what looked like a long wooden shaft with a spearhead. I wasn't sure whether he had seen us; I hoped he hadn't. Then I spotted another man, and yet another. I whispered to Mimi, "Do you've a pair of scissors or anything sharp? They're armed."

"Why on earth would I be carrying a pair of scissors to a picnic, Rohan?"

"I don't know; women always have everything in their purses."

"Well, I'm not that type of woman."

I couldn't see her face clearly; but from her voice, I could make out that she was nervous too. We were both on edge. I immediately extended my right hand; Mimi grabbed it and tightened her grip.

Obviously, I didn't want to argue with her. I told her to stay put. "I'll go look for a wooden pole or something."

"How can you fight so many guys?"

"I don't know, but I have to try, right?"

"I think I figured out what they said," Mimi whispered. "But you know my Hokkien is rusty; so I may be wrong."

Still, I was curious. "What did they say?"

"One of them said, 'Here's a big one.'. . . Maybe they've seen you," she said, indicating my six-foot height.

"I don't think so; they're guessing." It was quite dark on our side; moreover, we were under the shadows, and much closer to the bushes. Suddenly, I stumbled over a dead tree branch about five feet long. I quickly picked it up, and sat down next to Mimi. I immediately started pulling off the dry leaves and the smaller branches. I knew it wasn't the perfect weapon, but it was better than nothing. Meanwhile, Mimi took off her jewelry and asked me to keep it safe in my pocket, because chances were they would be targeting her purse first.

At that point, we thought of calling the police. However, to our surprise, there was no signal. I muttered, "How is that possible? We're hardly two hundred yards away from the parking lot." I didn't want to waste any more time. "Well, let's walk back slowly through the bushes, and when they see us out in the open, it won't be more than a hundred yards to our car. We can try to make a run for it from there."

But to our surprise, we found the low land connecting that small place to the main beach was completely flooded, and I had no idea how deep the water might be. We always sat on the promenade whenever we came here before. And who knew there would be a high tide at this hour? I cursed myself: why did I bring Mimi here? That's when we saw at least four or five men wearing nothing but shorts; and all of them had long spears in their hands. They looked like Indonesian Chinese – well-built and of short height. The water was right below their waist level.

I suddenly remembered that a couple of guys had murdered a girl a few years before on reclaimed land not so far from there; and I finally understood why the Singapore police constantly advertised, 'Low crime doesn't mean no crime.' I grabbed the branch tighter, though I knew the rotten wood was nothing compared to their sharp spearheads. I tried to remember every trick I had learned in close combat training during my national service. I asked Mimi whether she would be able to go through the water if I could hold off those guys for a couple of minutes.

"That's ridiculous; I can't leave you here and run," Mimi answered softly but firmly.

"Then what do you suggest we do?"

"Get me something, maybe slightly smaller. We'll fight them together."

But as I bent down to pick up another wooden branch, one of the men asked Mimi something in Hokkien.

Mimi answered hesitantly and slowly. The guys all laughed out loud and spoke to each other in Hokkien. Their contempt and mockery made my blood boil in anger; I clenched my teeth. They asked her something again, this time, in fluent Mandarin, and she answered them. I had no clue what was going on; I decided to wait for the outcome of the discussion and then strike.

After a few minutes Mimi turned back to me and said, "Please drop the shaft, and let's go back."

"Are you kidding me? Go back where?"

"The place where we were sitting."

"What did they say?"

"Come on, I'll tell you everything. After all, you're my hero."

At Mimi's persistence, I went back and sat down, though quite reluctantly. Then she leaned forward and kissed me. Mimi had spent a good part of her life in Sydney; she was more generous with her kisses and affections than average Singaporean girls.

Turned out, there was no real danger; those guys had been fishing. There had been a high tide and that had flooded the lowland and brought in loads of fishes as well.

I suddenly woke up at Lisa's question. "Dad, when are we going to set the birds free?"

"I guess now is as good a time as any. Let's play a game first."

I took out a few pencils and notepads and said to Lisa and Matthew, "Listen, you guys know that your mother and I have been married for ten years and now we have decided to live our lives separately. That's no big deal, and we're really proud of you guys for not making it one. Also, you must've noticed a few changes in our daily lives. But you know what, changes are good. And in the middle of all these changes, there's one thing permanent: our love for each other. No matter what, we'll always live under one sky and we'll always love you guys more than anything."

I looked at Mimi. She kept quiet the whole time; she didn't say anything, but she smiled at me, possibly, to show her appreciation. It was a difficult subject to talk about, but we both knew that it was better to have it in the open than leaving it unsaid.

I continued, "Now each of us will write our best memory from each year; and then, we'll select one from all four, and attach that message to one beautiful bird and let it fly away as our best family memory of the year. That way, whenever or wherever we see the open sky, we'll fondly remember all our beautiful memories; and these birds will be carrying them forever from one person to the other."

Everyone became quite excited; Matthew, Lisa, and even Mimi clapped in a show of appreciation, and Lisa circled us twice in a fit of excitement. I was glad to see a smile on everyone's face.

I raised both my hands to draw their attention. "Well, let's get down to business, people. The year would be 1996, when it all started."

Lisa and Matthew cried out loud, "Dad, we weren't even born in 1996. Not fair."

I had anticipated this might happen, and I was prepared. "Soon you guys will study history at school, and you'll have to answer questions about things that had happened a hundred or thousand years ago. Now we're talking about events that took place maybe six or seven years before you're born. You've heard our stories and must've seen all our family videos; pick your favorite moments from there. If your mother and I can't top that, then your choice will stand."

As soon as I laid out the rules of the game, everybody got down to scribbling their best memories of 1996. Choosing the most memorable event of the first year of our family was easy; our first date was the obvious choice for everyone.

With the evening approaching, the birds were getting impatient to get out. I carefully opened the cage and took out a colorful hummingbird. Everyone stood up with their glasses in hand and cheered. And with that chosen message, I let go the bird and it quickly disappeared into the trees.

The 1997 suggestion came from Mimi: "It gotta be the Changi Beach picnic." Yes, we remembered that picnic for many reasons. Mimi always said, "That picnic had sealed the deal for us," and she knew that we would be a good team. Matthew and Lisa had heard about it; the story itself was good enough to sell, and we made another unanimous decision. But before I could take out a bird from the cage, Matthew suddenly asked, "I don't understand one thing, though: why did you guys go sit there in the dark, and not up here on the dry beach?"

Mimi and I looked at each other. We smiled and decided to let it go unanswered.

Lisa jumped up, clapped her hands, and said, "Wow, Dad, this is fun. I want to fly the next one." But before anybody could even scribble a suggestion for 1998, Lisa screamed on top of her voice, "It must be the wedding."

"But that happened in 1999, Dear," Mimi corrected Lisa, and she continued, "Indeed, something hilarious happened in 1998." Then she narrated an incident the kids had never heard before. She said, "One Sunday morning, when your father came to pick me up, he accidentally met my dad. When he knocked at the door, my father was in the living room cleaning an old rifle. As you know, no one keeps a rifle at home in Singapore; it was an antique piece. So, when he answered the door, my dad had that gun in his hand. And not knowing what was going on, your father took that as my father's total disapproval of the relationship. The gun really scared him, and all that came out of his mouth was 'Wrong house, sir, I apologize,' and he ran like hell. The rest is obviously history."

The kids burst into laughter. I made a feeble protest: "No, I didn't run." But no one was listening; the kids were busy savoring their dad's momentary weakness.

One by one we remembered all the other important events in our family—our wedding, Lisa and Matthew's first birthdays, their first school days, and more, and every time, with the same ritual, we freed those memories from the confines of our family home to fly away and stay alive in the big universe for years to come. Slowly the evening fell on us, but it was a day in our family that possibly no one would ever forget. We felt closer than ever; we stayed there for a little while longer, lying side by side and each one holding the next person's hand.

When I drove them all back home, Matthew and Lisa were so tired that they both dozed off in the car. But Lisa woke up, hugged me, and whispered, "Best picnic ever. Thank you, Dad."

Mimi thanked me as well. However, before she left the car, she asked, "What're you going to do with the cage now?"

"I guess I have to throw it away."

"Let's keep it; give it to me."

Chapter 16

AFTER ARRIVING IN THAILAND, I immediately got myself settled at Chalong Beach in Phuket. It was a beautiful choice, far away from the hustle and bustle of Phuket's tourist crowd—in between the famous Patong Beach and the farther-south Rawai Beach. The place was quiet and had a nice, clean environment—a convenient hideaway for solitary activities. In the last few days before coming here, I had imagined myself writing for hours with a cup of coffee on the deck of my beachfront apartment; and now, as I arranged a corner for my writing, I followed that picture in my head as closely as possible.

In an effort to kick-start my new career, I set myself a strict routine, with the intention of reviewing my progress after every six months. I woke up in the morning at six o'clock; and after a jog, shower, and breakfast, I sat down with my laptop for at least four to five hours. Meanwhile, I quickly picked up two regular columns from financial publishers I had occasionally contributed to earlier. I was glad, because that'd obviously help me keep my monthly expenses covered. But column writing was easy; I was more concerned with the fiction I wanted to create.

I was new to fiction writing, so I accepted slow progress at first. But it seemed as though every time I opened my laptop, my thoughts froze like an ice sculpture. When I did write a couple of pages, they sounded incredibly wonderful at first; but with time they melted into nothing but water. The razor-thin edges and the sharp lines quickly vanished into thin air for lack of any solid substance.

After four months of blank pages, I finally shut down my laptop in disgust. I couldn't help thinking that average guys like me don't write great fictions; they fill in pages. Then what was the point of writing? I had a couple of ideas, but none came out as eye-popping as I had expected. I wrote, rewrote, deleted, and wrote again. Still I had nothing.

When I realized I was miserably failing at writing anything good, instead of wasting more time on it, I decided to concentrate on finding a purpose in my life. After all, that's what had brought me there in the first place. If I ever got to know my role in the universe, I could as happily follow that course. Maybe writing fiction wasn't my thing and I was supposed to do other things instead. But unfortunately there also felt like a big sign of failure staring me in the eye. Was it all in vain? Many would say it was, indeed, a stupid idea, leaving everything in search of something that I didn't even know where to look for. But I was sure, as Mr. Barco said, that the answer to all my questions was right under my nose. I guess I just couldn't see it.

I closed my eyes and tried to remember if I had missed anything. When I was a child, I used to look at the ocean for hours—how the ripples on the distant horizon slowly swelled into waves and came crashing down on the shore. Each wave had a character - different from the previous one or the next. Waves that didn't have much strength quickly cascaded down in front of my feet; but others were high and looked ferocious—their crests curled and fell over other advancing waves with thunderous sounds. But in the end they all rapidly culminated in the same thing, creating an incredible bond between the waves and the sea. The waves remained peaceful for a while amid unity and amity, then playfully separated again to create a million other waves to wash away a bit of sand every time. This eternal fight between the sea and the coastline had always fascinated me; as a kid, I wondered how the Goa coastline survived when the water kept constantly washing away its sand into the sea.

In life, aren't most of us as average as the zillions of sand grains on a sea beach? Then, what holds everything all together? What gives us the impetus to stand up in the face of adversity? Like sand on a beach, at times, we all get washed away by the daily grind, but we fight back and stand on our feet again. Does this continuous struggle make us more robust? Do our problems make us more resilient? The thing is, nothing vanishes into thin air here; and as Mr. Barco said, there are many things happening around us that we simply don't notice. One sand grain may not look like much to us, but together they're strong and make an invincible, indispensable force that protects beaches or becomes part of the concrete we use to build our houses. So, even a sand grain has a purpose in existence.

What then is my purpose in life? I thought, I eat because I feel hungry; I sleep because I feel sleepy; I seek company because I feel lonely; but why do I live? No doubt my ambition in life gave me a reason to live; but that in itself couldn't explain why I was here in the first place. I guess we all can exist in our standalone capacity like one individual sand grain or one wave, or stay together on a beach and share good and bad times.

But who am I, or what am I? Am I Rohan Fernandez or just another human being, like one of so many waves in the ocean? What's my role here in the universe? Like each sand grain must protect a beach or build concrete, I must also have a purpose here. And as each sand grain is different from the others in shape, color, and size, I must be different as well from other human beings.

I remembered when I had asked Mr. Barco the same questions: "How am I any different from others, and how do I leave my identification mark here?"

But Mr. Barco had the simplest of all explanations: "Why do you think all our thumbprints are different? Our hair, skin, and eyes have one color or the other. Even human blood is classified into few types. Although it's difficult, we can still find a matching heart or a kidney. But can you find a matching thumbprint? Nature doesn't create something so unique for no reason. Each thing we see around us has a purpose. It can only mean that we're born to be different and we're born to leave our own identification mark in this world—one way or another. There are special attributes inherent in all of us. We have to find out what we're good at; everyone has distinct characteristics in them."

But what was that special thing for me? At first, I had thought it could be writing; but if I couldn't write anything, how on earth was that possible? I sincerely wanted an answer—any answer. If the answer to everything was under my nose, then I wanted to see it right away.

I always had thought life was particularly difficult for average people. They think they can do a lot of things, but they're often constrained by lack of talent. Mr. Barco insisted that there are no ordinary people, and his arguments were rock solid, yet, I had difficulty accepting myself as anything but ordinary. I still needed to justify my existence. Mr. Barco said my being here couldn't be without a reason. Then, who am I and what am I doing here?

I looked up; everything appeared dull and pale. The vast ocean in front of me, the sky, and the trees looked dead and ridiculously stagnant, as if framed in a still picture. We tend to love nature because it's always so dynamic; it changes in the blink of an eye. Now that the dynamism was gone, the beauty had evaporated as well. I knew something was terribly wrong.

I got up from my chair and walked up and down the balcony, faster and faster, until my head started spinning from circling the small space. An inexplicable spasm rose from my chest, swirling and twisting its way to my brain. My hands and feet became numb, my vision grew blurred, and I started to perspire profusely. I felt like throwing up.

But I also wanted to go on; I wanted something to happen—anything. I finally grabbed the side rail as I fell on my knees. With my hands on the railing, I crawled back up to my chair and sat down. Isolation and emptiness surrounded me. I could hardly breathe; I felt a void in my heart. Suddenly, I heard Lisa screaming in the distance, as though she and Matthew were fighting again. It got louder. I stood up and looked around; there's no sign of anyone. I must've been hallucinating. I forgot that I wasn't a part of their daily lives anymore. I had left my old Singapore life for good.

I wiped my eyes and took a sip of my coffee. I missed my home in Singapore; I missed Matthew and Lisa. Had I thrown away my comfortable and apparently happy life in Singapore for nothing?

Or more importantly, was I really happy then? I knew I wasn't; all my happiness evaporated since the third or fourth year of our marriage. The thing is, looking happy and being happy are two different things. I was busy looking good in other people's eyes: a good job, a great wife, and an affluent lifestyle—absolutely the right image for any successful executive. How shallow was that? But what had happened? And what changed the old Rohan into a new one?

One thing became clear: when I was a little boy, everything was either black or white, but once I grew up, everything became gray. But when did all that happen? I wasn't sure; though, I knew it'd taken place over a long period of time. Like we don't notice our many physical changes even if we look in the mirror every day, I didn't notice when and how I'd turned into a materialistic snob.

Our minds always play games with us; that's how the same thing looks different at two different times, and from two different angles. As much as we admire objective thinking, maybe that's a concept as oxymoronic as virtual reality. Like one person can't be physically present on both sides of a table at one point of time, they also can't take a mental picture from both positions at the same time.

The mind constantly helps us justify our actions—good or bad. Otherwise, how does a thief who is a loving father and a devoted family man break into a stranger's house and steal his belongings? In his mind, he must have his reasons, or else his mind wouldn't allow him to go through with such a repugnant action. His reason may be poverty, in which case he may think that he's every right to fend for his family and do whatever it takes to feed them three square meals. Or maybe he's simply playing Robin Hood. That we'll never know without getting into his head.

Now, I sensed that I was looking at life the whole time from a totally different angle than I had as a child. Whenever I had doubts, my mind tricked me into seeing and believing only the part I wanted to see. The rest became nonexistent. Society created a bubble and named it Exclusive, and I ran after it, be it a club membership or a social group. I thought that by being a part of that elite class, I would automatically become part of the chosen few and would no longer be ordinary. The tags kept coming—Private, Select, Limited—and I fell victim every time. Who wouldn't know that these were merely words and wouldn't mean a thing? Only the vulnerable ones; and we all become vulnerable at one time or another.

I remembered what Mr. Barco had told me in Lauterbrunnen: it's, indeed, the society that builds and fuels our ego. He was right. I also remembered what he had said about how we could live life without getting too involved in the materialistic world. I must learn to live as if it's an act, he said. Today, if I was given to play the role of an unsuccessful writer, so be it; I needed to do my best. One day, if that writer found success, and I got to play that role too, that would be another thing.

I immediately went to the bathroom and repeatedly splashed cold water on my face. I came back to the balcony and closed my eyes for a while. I could hear the sound of the roaring sea again. Soon, I felt a lot better, and when I opened my eyes this time, I could see everything clearly. The view from the deck was, indeed, splendid. The beach in Phuket was very different from that of Singapore. That part of the Andaman Sea in Phuket was also pretty rough at times, but that gave it character.

Nature has the unique ability to cheer us up anytime, any day of the year. It unfolds new mysteries every day. We can look at the same sea for days, weeks, and months, and it can still retain its vivacious and sparkling, yet ever-mysterious beauty. We can look at the same set of trees for years, yet their beauty and charisma can overpower us every time. We may see the same hills, slopes, bends, and bushes again and again, but they never fail to stir us up even for the hundredth time. Perhaps nature has a soothing effect on us because it makes no demands on us. It was there, it is there now, and it will still be there even we decide to come back at a later date. And that sets the mind at peace. In urban life, everything has become a now-or-never; we're always on a schedule we dare not miss. Whereas nature gives us freedom, not because it can give us more space to run free; it's because it allows the mind to run free.

However, amid all this freedom, there's a very subtle logic and a profound routine in nature. Everything happens on time, every time, and 'round the clock; yet the transitions are smooth and as easy as day and night. I reckoned I needed a routine, where transitions would be easy and not forced and abrupt like the regimented kind I started with in Phuket.

I spent the next few days taking all this in and putting everything back in perspective. I didn't know whether I should be happy or sad. I hadn't made any progress with my fiction writing since I had started. But I had made a little progress in making peace with myself.

And as time went by, I slowly felt better and was able to concentrate again. I remembered once Mr. Barco quoted a wise man as saying, "The more you walk toward the east, you fundamentally get farther away from the west." Then he'd explained what the wise man really meant: "When someone leans toward spiritualism, the person automatically loses interest in a materialistic world."

Indeed, the moment I could dream about a future in writing, I felt disengaged with the rest. My initial boredom and the pain of lonesome Friday nights in a bar vanished with the appearance of a new goal in sight. I recognized that we often get bored when we don't have a goal or we can't visualize the end result. If an aspiring Olympian is looking at a gold medal at the end of every fourth year, that person naturally loses sight of the normal 365-day cycle. They will then live for every Olympic year—their year starts and ends only at the end of every fourth year. Weekend fun or normal year-end festivities will have little or no meaning for them. The Olympic days are their Christmas and New Year.

At first, I had thought I was losing valuable time. In the last few months, I had done nothing but ruminate over my failed life. However, analyzing my past had also helped me get clarity. Maybe struggling is like plowing the land. The better we plow, the higher the yield. The only way to get any success in my writing was to keep trying. I bolted myself to my seat again, determined to work until something good popped up. But it still felt like I was swimming in a vast ocean, with no sight of shores on any side.

A few weeks later, I saw a flicker of hope, though it wasn't from the lighthouse I was looking for. I received a welcome distraction – a Skype call - from Ade. "What're you doing in the first week of December?"

I felt alive. Apart from my interactions with the cleaning lady in my apartment, and at my routine lunch and dinner at the nearby restaurants, I hadn't had any genuine, sincere human contacts in weeks. I was truly vulnerable. Like any desperate man in the sea, I would've grabbed any help. I was lucky it was Adeline.

"Wanna go to New Zealand? My sis had given birth to a baby girl; I'm going to see her. In that case you don't have to fly to Vienna again to talk to me; you can make up or break up with me there."

"Who said I wanted to break up?"

"No one. But you never made up, either."

"How can one make up from more than five thousand miles away?"

"Well, then get ready for the best make-up sex ever."

I didn't want to prolong that conversation. We arranged to meet at Christchurch at her sister's place; then we would take her sister's car and drive to Queenstown. I had never been there, but I had heard so much about that place; people say it's one of the most scenic spots in the southern hemisphere. I told Ade that I would take care of booking us a place there.

"Yay! We're going on our honeymoon!"

"We're going on vacation."

"Think what you want to. I gotta go."

I knew that any argument with Ade was pretty much useless. It might sound like bullying to anyone, but I knew there was one difference: Ade could back off as easily as she advanced. Everything she asked for was more like a child's wish. If you gave in, the child would be happy; if you didn't, the child would forget in no time and would occupy herself with other things. That flexibility gave her a childlike innocence in an adult body. She held no grudges whatsoever; she would wipe it out of her memory.

I thought that could be one way of living; indeed, a good way. We certainly cannot expect to get everything we aspire to in life; some things we'll get, and some we won't. But that doesn't mean we must stop hoping altogether. In fact, we should celebrate what we get in life, and we should not only forget what we didn't achieve; we should also forget we ever wanted it. Maybe that's one reason childhood can be the happiest time in our lives. How did Ade do it? It always seemed so effortless; it was like she had never left her childhood. The complications of life never touched her.

There was a time when I didn't care what other people thought about me, either. I never thought of owning a Mercedes or a BMW; I didn't even know the difference between a big house and a townhouse. But back then, I was a happy boy roaming around the countryside with my own thoughts, losing my mind in my own world.

Chapter 17

DECEMBER FINALLY CAME in due time, though I thought it took longer than usual. I was so looking forward to my summer in New Zealand that each day seemed like a drag, especially with my unproductive, monotonous routine.

I knew much of the initial awkwardness with Adeline was over, but I still wanted to apologize and explain myself personally. While waiting, I tried to concentrate on my writing, but I didn't achieve much, thanks to my restless mind. With every passing day I missed her more.

We were supposed to meet at the airport and then go see her sister for a while before driving off to Queenstown later that day. I had already booked a serviced apartment facing the beautiful Wakatipu Lake in Queenstown. If the pictures on the website was anything to go by, the place looked heavenly. I felt exited. I knew this trip would be different. At least, there wouldn't be a long list of social calls, and no judging eyes. I could barely wait.

I landed in Christchurch right on time; it was eleven thirty in the morning. Christchurch was never as busy as Auckland or other major city airports, so everything cleared pretty fast. However, as I headed out of the baggage claim area, I noticed someone holding a welcome sign with my name on it. I paused for a second and wondered what could've happened to Ade. She was fine when I had spoken with her the night before, and her flight was supposed to land two hours before mine. Had she already left for her sister's house? That would be quite unlike her, though. While I was busy thinking of every unpleasant possibility that came to my head, Adeline's face suddenly popped up from behind the placard.

"Ade?" I gulped.

The moment she noticed I had already seen her, she threw away the placard and ran toward me; and to my surprise, from about five feet away, she jumped into my arms, wrapped her legs around my waist, and kissed me. I wasn't quite ready for this sudden euphoria. I dropped my luggage in reflex and fortunately managed to grab her in time. Ade was no lightweight petite lady. Fortunately, I was strong enough for the impact. Everyone started clapping; I was terribly embarrassed. I'd had no idea that we had an audience, too. But Ade stepped down and gracefully bowed to thank the onlookers.

"Are you crazy or what?" came out of my mouth, even before I could say 'hi' to her.

"Why?"

"You could've caused an accident now, and worse, you could've been hurt."

"Little accidents once in a while aren't so bad. It gets you a lot of attention, but not much pain. Who wouldn't like that?"

"And what about the name placard?"

"Oh, that? That's not mine; I took it from another guy. His visitor had already arrived, so he didn't need it anymore. I just put your name on the other side."

"But why?"

"I wasn't sure whether you would be able to recognize me after such a long time, especially when I've become so much prettier." She flipped her hair to draw my attention.

I noticed a difference in her hairstyle; it was slightly shorter and there were streaks of auburn nicely blended with her natural black hair. She definitely looked more flamboyant; the cut and the highlights suited her personality. "You look great; the hairstyle fits you. Anyway, what's the plan now?"

Ade squeezed my right hand tightly and kept walking. She informed me in the cab that we wouldn't be leaving for Queenstown that day. Instead, we would be spending the night at her sister's place. "Guess what, we're having a barbecue party tonight."

Obviously, it wasn't what I had wanted; but the surprise wasn't totally unexpected. I shrank inside at first at the mention of a party, but soon I recovered. I definitely couldn't avoid meeting people forever. Who knows, it might be nice to make friends again. Adeline had come to New Zealand to have a good time; and all relationships need understanding and compromise. My apologies to her in that case had to wait. I immediately looked at her and said, "That's a great idea."

In a short while, we reached her sister's two-story townhouse. The house was quite close to the city; Christchurch isn't very big, anyway. Her sister, Megan, opened the door and welcomed us, throwing her arms around Ade and saying, "Baby sis, you're finally here. I'm so happy." Ade introduced us both and rushed inside; I wasn't sure what the hurry was, but I followed Megan into the living room.

The house was quite spacious; there were two huge bedrooms downstairs with lots of sunlight, and the kitchen and living room were upstairs. The living room had a big, open floor plan with an easy flow to its southwest balcony. The overall look was contemporary and even avant-garde.

Suddenly I heard Ade's voice from the staircase: "Look who's here!" Ade reappeared from downstairs, holding a baby in her arms, and introduced her to me, "This is Piper."

Ade looked happy and pretty comfortable cuddling the baby, wrapped in pink. Her face lit up every time the baby made the slightest movement. She showered her with kisses as Piper wrapped her little fingers around Ade's forefinger. "Isn't she the prettiest little thing?" Ade didn't look anything like over the top animated girl I had met in Vienna.

Megan was incredibly warm and hospitable. Although the sisters had lot of similarities feature-wise, Megan was definitely more poised and composed than her younger sister. She told me that her husband, Lucas, would be back in the evening, and he was very anxious to meet me. Lucas was a New Zealander; they had met in Munich at an industrial exhibition, and had fallen in love.

Lucas insisted that we stay the night and drive to Queenstown the next morning. It would be a seven-hour drive and much better in the daylight, he said, especially for foreigners who wanted to enjoy the scenic beauty. Besides, he had also invited a couple of their friends for a very informal barbecue to celebrate Ade's first visit there. In fact, it was also the first party at their house since Piper was born.

Lucas was an excellent guy; he worked as general manager of a gaming software company. We quickly found we had a common interest in capital markets. Lucas had been working closely with his team to take the company public. Knowing that I had worked on many IPOs before, he was keen to discuss a few things with me. We spoke for about an hour until their friends started coming.

The evening was a refreshing change for me; turned out, Lukas and his friends were all in mid-thirties; I hadn't chatted with people my age for a long time.

There were two other couples that night: Lucas's sister Renee and her husband, Will; and friends of the family, Miranda and Jeff. They all looked like old friends and quite comfortable with each other. Surprisingly, I felt comfortable too.

Once Ade and I got to know everyone, the real fun started. I'd had no idea that Megan was such a great host. She looked at each detail and made sure that the party went on without a hitch. We all enjoyed the wine and the food—possibly a bit too much.

As soon as the party showed signs of fatigue, Megan was there to rescue it. "Who wants to play a game?"

"What kind of game? Hope there's not too much running around," quipped Miranda.

"In fact, there's none," Megan said. "It's more like a stand-up comedy thing. You have to tell us a funny story or create your own witty joke to make others laugh."

I didn't think I could come up with anything remotely funny. However, Megan stood up with her wine glass in hand and said, "Guys, don't worry too much. The most vital part of any stand-up comedy show is already here—we have an enthusiastic live audience. So, bring it on."

Adeline suddenly asked, "Do you want to split into teams? That might be more fun."

Everyone agreed this might be a good idea; at least this way we could've another person to lean on. Two teams were formed immediately: Megan, Lucas, Miranda, and Jeff on one side, and Renee, Will, Ade, and I on the opposite team.

Megan asked, "Who'll go first?"

Ade said, "Let's flip."

Meanwhile, Megan took out an hourglass from their games kit and said. "Each team will get sixty seconds to respond with their counter joke."

"Do we have to finish our joke within sixty seconds, or start responding within sixty seconds?" Renee wanted to clarify.

Megan confirmed that we had to start within sixty seconds. Our team won the toss, and Megan immediately turned the hourglass upside down; and the countdown began.

Who knew, what we had watched a million times and what always looked funny on the TV screen wasn't so simple after all; we were all scratching our heads. Utter silence dominated the room. However, with ten seconds left on the clock, I cleared my throat and said, "Well, can anyone tell me why dinner guests aren't supposed to put their elbows on the table? Let's be honest with ourselves: is eating with your elbows hanging out all the time more comfortable than resting them on the table? I'll tell you why; because it'll make your guests so comfortable that they'll never want to leave."

Everyone burst out laughing. "Wow! Where did that come from?" asked Adeline in a surprised voice.

Frankly, I was a bit surprised myself; I guess it was the old competitive spirit that manifested itself in a time of dire need.

However, she didn't want to give her opponent team any extra time. She immediately turned the hourglass and told Megan, "It's your turn."

One after another, each person came through with mind-blowing pieces. The evening turned out quite entertaining and full of witty jokes and laughter. But as time passed, the game became more intense and more and more competitive, at least, between the two rival team captains. The sisters clearly didn't want to give each other any extra time. What had started out as party fun soon turned into sibling rivalry. Ade and Megan were at each other's throats. Later, Lucas told me that their rivalry hadn't started that evening, but had been like this since their childhood. Now that they had grown up, they had learned to live with each other's differences. Although the sibling rivalry didn't come out in the open very often, I guess their many differences still bothered them.

Maybe Lucas had some idea about how to handle this; he quickly pushed his drink aside, stood up, and said, "Time out. . . time out."

"I already turned the clock; so if you guys want time out, you have to call it before the next turn," responded Megan.

Twenty seconds were already gone in deliberation; but Ade was the last person to admit defeat. "No worries, I'm not gonna give them the satisfaction of winning this." She looked at me, and then continued. "I don't understand how come playing with someone is actually playing, and walking with someone means walking, but sleeping with someone means quite another thing? On the contrary, there may be no sleeping involved at all. Is it only me? Or are you puzzled too?"

We all raised our glasses. We were so busy competing that none had noticed the empty glasses. Lucas quickly went to the bar to fix the whiskeys; I poured the wine.

Surprisingly, as soon as the game ended, both sisters behaved like nothing had happened. When I looked at Lucas, he blankly looked at me and said, "Don't ask me; I don't get it either."

The party went on till two-thirty in the morning, and that night I got a taste of what I had been missing since I had left Singapore. The whole night I didn't even think once about my writing or my purpose in life; I moved with the flow. And I liked it for a change. I was glad I had come with Adeline.

Chapter 18

THE NEXT MORNING, Ade and I started out early immediately after breakfast, but not before we promised Megan and Lucas that we would spend more time in Christchurch on our way back. All in all, I had spent less than twenty-four hours in their house, but I had fallen in love with that family. Megan and Lucas were not only good hosts, they were also great fun to spend time with. However, as we drove off, I also felt happy; finally, I would be alone with Ade after such a long time. I had so much to say to her. Indeed, I had not been able to apologize to her yet for my actions in Vienna. I needed to get that off my chest on this trip.

About three hours later, we suddenly drove into an amazing scenic paradise; and the breathtaking view prompted me to pay respect to the landscape there. I stopped the car and got out, Ade following. We were spellbound. The color of the water in Lake Tekapo was pure turquoise blue, right out of a painter's palette. We later found out that the melted glaciers had made the water color so intense there.

From a distance Ade noticed a tiny church on the shore; we went in to take a look. There was something different about that church too. A couple of empty benches were lined up in two rows, and there were candleholders on large consoles on both sides of the wall. The big wooden cross wasn't fixed to a wall; it was kept standing on wooden planks in front of a huge window opening to the lake behind it. The moment I sat down, I experienced my life's best optical illusion: a big wooden cross floating upright on deep turquoise-blue water, without any support.

The mood inside was divine—more spiritual than religious. It looked like more than a Good Shepherd's wayside church; it offered rest to the restless, peace to the disturbed, solace to the grieving. I didn't see any priest there; but I could feel a vibrant energy at work.

For a while, I was oblivious to Ade's presence next to me. I guess I was busy making a connection with my own soul, and silence was the key. It had been a long time since I had felt that way—so close to my heart. For few seconds I lost any sense of gravity, as if my body was floating in the air, and I experienced absolute peace and tranquility in my mind.

Possibly Ade had her own realization too. We came out of the church and walked hand-in-hand for a while by the lakeside, saving it all in our memories: the experience at Lake Tekapo. We drove without a word for a long time. I didn't ask what her experience was like; I guess that would've been too personal. I always believed everyone needed personal space, and there're things in life that can only be felt and cherished within; no human language can interpret their intensity.

At about five o'clock in the evening, we reached our beautiful serviced apartment facing Lake Wakatipu. The place looked amazing, even better than those website pictures.

We had been driving the whole day, but we didn't feel particularly tired. Our little experience at the church had also rejuvenated us. After showering, we decided to take a walk to the city center and get a good dinner. The usher in the restaurant showed us a table outside, and I ordered a bottle of Moët & Chandon.

Ade asked, "What are we celebrating?"

"You."

"That's funny; you ran like hell last time you saw me, and now you're celebrating seeing me again?"

It felt like we were back to our Vienna days again. "Why's that funny? I don't see you complaining when the sun leaves every day and comes right back the next day to greet you good morning."

"What're you saying; you'll disappear again?"

We both laughed. Meanwhile, the waiter had come back with the champagne. The sight of a million bubbles trapped in a flute champagne glass—each one fighting to get past the other one to be on top first—can make anyone dizzy; and once you take the first sip after a long drive sitting next to the person you love, can send you reeling in a magic spell. I felt as if I were at Disneyland enjoying the rides; all my unpleasant thoughts and worries were kept neatly outside the boundaries.

An hour and a half, and a couple of drinks later, we both bounced back to life, our traveling weariness gone. We loved what Moet did to us; after all, alcohol does good things too. One hour before, we had been happy to take a slow walk to the town center; now we were ready to take on Queenstown. But we chose not to go to any casino or out barhopping that night; instead we decided to walk back to our apartment.

The sight from our balcony was amazing. It had a sweeping view of the lake surrounded by the Southern Alps. With the moonlight shining strong on the blue water, the lake looked calm and serene. The lights from the small houses at the foothills of the Remarkables mountain range encircled the lake. We pulled our bench a little closer to the edge of the balcony and sat with our feet up on the railing. Ade leaned on my shoulder. I pulled out my left arm, inched in closer, and stretched it out over her shoulders and made room for her to lean comfortably on my chest. We didn't say another word; we just sat there.

Most often when two people are in complete sync, words become superfluous. As her left fingers curled into mine, I shivered in excitement like a teenage boy and slowly pressed her soft warm body against mine. She looked up and pulled my head down to her lips. This time I didn't want to break away; it all felt so right.

* * *

The next morning we both woke up late. The sun was shining bright and strong, though there were traces of water on the deck, indicating that it might have rained a little earlier. Ade was still lying on the bed, leaning against the pillows and covering herself with a milky-white comforter in one hand; so I got up and made coffee for both of us.

Ade said, "Thank you, but you didn't have to do that."

"Who would've done that, princess?" I asked as I sat next to the small writing table.

"No one. We're on our honeymoon, remember?"

I looked at her curiously. Ade had a naughty look in her face as she asked, "You prefer coffee to me?" She smiled. . . and then, suddenly dropped the comforter to her lap and pulled it back over her head faster than I could blink. I jumped up from the chair, put my coffee on a side table, and pulled the drapes.

Needless to say, we didn't do anything that tourists do in Queenstown, even though Ade religiously picked up the tour brochures every time we went out for lunch and dinner. There's a lot to do in the city: skydiving, bungee jumping, wine tasting, the Milford Sound trip, and other day tours to some of the most scenic places on earth. They always seemed like great ideas for the next morning; but definitely not good enough to waste that particular moment in time.

But then the next morning, Ade would make fun of each one of those brochures. She said, "Tell me, what's so great about bungee jumping? And who the hell in a sound mind jumps down from four hundred feet, trusting a sling to hold their weight? And skydiving? Come on, is there really such a thing? That has been reserved for the birds for ages. Diving to your death from above 20,000 feet is not definitely skydiving; it's more like a death wish to me."

The next day, she picked up a wine-tasting brochure and said, "Good deal? . . . Seriously? We can buy a few bottles of Chardonnay with this money and get drunk without going anywhere. It doesn't sound like a great deal to me."

After a while she turned serious and said, "Don't you think we can do all these on our own when we're no longer together? Why waste time now?"

I agreed; and we didn't go out that day either. Truthfully, we were happy where we were, and we were trying to hold on to that feeling as long as we could. Indeed, I was so happy that I didn't even want to bring up the Vienna incident just yet. And to my surprise, the constant chaos in my head had also cooled down. Why was that? Was it the Adeline effect? But I didn't want to think about that either.

However, even before we noticed the passage of time, our last day in Queenstown arrived. We hadn't been anywhere but a few restaurants and our own room. So, we drove around a little to get a feel of the place, and finally landed up in Arrowtown—best known as New Zealand's gold rush town. It was a quaint little spot tucked in the foothills of the Remarkables, only a twenty-minute drive from Queenstown.

Both Ade and I were awestruck as soon as we arrived. Ade stopped in the middle of the road, looked to her right and to her left, and then wrapped her arms around me and said, "Awesome!"

I was speechless myself; I had never seen anything like this in my lifetime. It was as if we had traveled back in time.

The whole town looked like a movie set from an early twentieth-century Hollywood film; it had small wooden houses, horse carriages, antique streetlights, red telephone booths, and the traditional saloons we all had seen in Western movies. The museum had captured the town's gold mining history in great detail, and the trickling Arrow River in the summertime and the pine tree–lined cobblestone streets made the town a scenic beauty.

After visiting the museum, we wandered around for an hour, exploring the beauty and the silence along the Arrow River. The town also had its own charm: quiet neighborhoods, empty streets, alfresco dining, and lots of nicely decorated shops on Buckingham Street, selling New Zealand's finest clothing and souvenirs. I bought a scarf for Ade; she quickly wrapped it around herself to ward off the breeze from a recent, odd cold snap.

"See, it goes so well with my dress. Doesn't it? I love baby blue—my favorite."

By then we also felt hungry, and we slowly walked into a nice French restaurant on Ramshaw Lane. It had a delightful setting out in the open, surrounded by sycamores and oaks and a view of the Remarkables. I ordered a bottle of Albert Boxler Riesling while Ade looked through the menu. We both agreed that Arrowtown had carved a special place in our hearts.

I raised my glass. "Cheers!" She raised her glass and cheered as well, but not as instantaneously as I'd have expected of Ade. There was definitely something missing: her usual spontaneity and enthusiasm. What could she be thinking? I didn't want to wait to find out. "What's wrong?"

"Well, you know what, one thing still puzzles me. Could you please tell me why you left Vienna that day without saying anything? . . . No good-byes? . . . Nothing? But if you don't want to talk about it, I can respect that too."

"No, we can talk. In fact, in the last few days, there were so many times I wanted to speak with you about that, but there was never a good time. We were having so much fun that I didn't want to interrupt. I'm glad you brought it up. I'm sorry."

"I'm not exactly looking for an apology, you know. Was there any reason?"

A minute ago I had thought I was ready; in fact, I had thought I was ready ever since I'd decided to meet her here. I knew it was confession time, but I simply choked. Nothing came out of my mouth. Was I afraid of losing her?

I looked at her; and she looked at me inquisitively. I said, "But I really don't know where to start."

"Well, if I remember correctly, you said in Vienna that you loved Mimi, but you were not in love with her anymore, didn't you?" She paused for a while and took a sip from her wine glass. "Don't you want to move on? Don't you want to live in the present?" Ade seemed unable to suppress her curiosity.

"It's not about Mimi; it's about Lisa and Matthew," I blurted out even before she finished.

"What about Lisa and Matthew?"

I explained how I had worried that any other relationship might push them to second place in my heart. "I don't think I'm ready for that."

"No one will ever be ready for that. In fact, that's an awful thought. What makes you think I would want that? Don't you know that the human heart has many compartments? I'm only a medical student, so don't trust me. Go ask any heart surgeon. There're four chambers in our heart, but that's just human anatomy; I'm sure there're similar compartments for love and emotions as well. Otherwise, how can you love your parents, your spouse, and your kids all the same, and at the same time?"

She looked at me and continued. "Besides, love is not a game to me; so there's no competition. There can't be a first, second, or third place. Love is for one person to give to another without any consideration. I believe that's why people say true love is unconditional; I think it's more like an act of charity, because when we're in love, we give away our most precious thing: our hearts. If I love you, I must love you without expecting you to love me back; if you happen to love me that would be your act of charity."

I was lost for a minute. How could her definition of love echo the same message my dad had passed on to me years before: 'True love isn't about winning or losing.' Do all wise people really think alike? Of course, love isn't a ball game, or for that matter, any game; there's no coaching, and there're no practice sessions, and you can't chalk out a strategy to win anyone's love. All we have in love are two unprotected hearts in an open field. And that's why our hearts bleed so much when we get hurt. The fact is, Adeline was right: even if our hearts bleed, it's not always a lose-lose situation. The sanctity of love makes it all worth the pain; and that feeling is always our own, and we can hold on to that.

I pulled my chair closer and said, "I get your point. But I don't want them to feel anything but my number one priority."

"I get that; and I wouldn't want it any other way. You've your parental responsibility, and I'm glad you are up for the challenge. It says a lot about you."

"I don't know about that; but thank you."

Ade put down her wine glass at one side and stretched her right arm across the table in an effort to reach mine. My left hand met her halfway. She held my hand tightly and said, "I'm not asking you to marry me; in fact, I'm not asking for anything. Don't get me wrong, I love kids; but I don't want to have my own. I think there're plenty of them running around who need care and attention."

"You're absolutely right."

Ade continued, "After I finish my medical school in Vienna, I wanna do my residency in Germany or in Switzerland. Once I become a doctor, I would love to go and practice in Africa, Bangladesh or in India - places where doctors are most needed. Possibly, we'll be away from each other most of the time. But that doesn't mean we can't have feelings for each other, does it? Would that be really so wrong?"

"There's nothing wrong with that, Ade. But I also have one more prickly issue you might not know."

"What now? You like another girl or what?"

"Can you ever be serious for a minute?" I leaned back against my chair and told her that I wanted to explain why I had left my previous job.

"I don't need to know that," was her quick answer.

But now I had learned better. If we intended to go forward together, I didn't want to run in parallel lines anymore; we needed to know everything about each other. I said, "No, you must; it's important," and then, I told her the gist of it: how the previous job could've been a wrong career choice for me, and why I wanted to pursue a future in writing.

"Well, that sounds good to me."

"No, it's not; I didn't write a damn thing in last six months since I had left my office. Now I only do small columns here and there, but nothing so far in fiction writing."

"Fiction writing takes time. I heard people say they took ten years to write their first novel."

Maybe that was true; but I didn't have the luxury of time. I couldn't wait ten years for this to happen or not happen. I looked blankly at the empty afternoon road and then decided to share my thoughts with her; maybe she could be of help. "But I don't know if I can wait that long; I need to know whether I can do this damn thing or not in another six months. Otherwise, I might have to find another job."

"But why would you go back to a job you don't like? What's wrong with trying this until you get it right? Besides, you want to give yourself six months, right? Then why worry now? Anything can happen by then."

"Yes, that's exactly what I want to do; try hard for the next six months. And that's where you come in."

"Me? How do I fit in the picture? I'm nobody to you, remember?"

"Apparently not anymore."

"So, what're you saying? Now we're together?"

I kept quiet. I didn't even know how to define what we had there. I remembered what my father had said long time before, 'Love has no logic.' Maybe, we should let it play out on its own, and see where that would take us. For now, we both wanted to concentrate on our work. Besides, life also taught me that in love, the next move isn't necessarily always a step up. I definitely didn't want to hurt her; but I also didn't want to rush into anything this time. We both liked the way it was. So, why kill a good thing going? Unconsciously, I nodded.

"Well, that takes care of another piece in my big jigsaw puzzle for now. Let's see how that fits; I'll let you know." Adeline raised her glass and then leaned back. She looked calm and poised; that hairstyle really suited her. It gave her face an instant character. My eyes met hers, and she smiled. She said, "I hope your puzzles work out too."

"Thank you. But the pieces are still all over the place; I'm working on it, though."

I wished I had good news for her. Even after a few months of soul searching, I finally had few clues, but nothing concrete yet. "The funny thing is, every time I look back a couple of years from today in search of the wrong pieces, I can't even understand how I had put in those pieces in the first place," I said. "They were so wrong, and it was so obvious. Why didn't I see that?"

"I guess we all go through different phases in life, make mistakes, and grow up. Nonetheless, it's an experience; and maybe we can learn one or two things from that."

"I guess you're right. Now that I can't reverse it, there's no point in brooding over that."

"Absolutely! Now go do your things: find your answers, and write your novel."

"I intend to do just that. And thank you." I folded my hands and bowed my head to show gratitude in a classic Singapore style.

Adeline laughed and then said, "Don't thank me; thank your girlfriend."

"And who would that be?"

"You'll see her later tonight. I have taken the liberty of calling her, and she has agreed to meet you and knock your socks off. She told me that it's gonna be a long night; she plans on revealing the best of Victoria's Secret tonight. So, I'll understand if you want to head back home now."

Chapter 19

AFTER I RETURNED from New Zealand in mid-December, I felt energized. I was ready to start again. I planned a simple routine this time and set that in motion the very next day. I needed to know that I had done everything in my power to make it work before I moved on to do anything else. But a week later, as I read through the first few pages of the manuscript again, I found something profoundly missing: honesty. The whole story had passed me by. I felt totally disconnected from the plot. I stared at the screen for nearly an hour, and after a lot of deliberation, pressed the delete button.

When I had left my six-figure job, I had thought writing was my true calling. But slowly, days had merged into weeks, weeks into months, and months into a half a year, and I still had nothing, but now I finally understood why. At first, when I had started writing, I thought I would be able to write novels like I used to write short stories before. But there was an obvious difference: the short stories I wrote back then all came from my heart and were part of my own life, but when I started writing fiction this time, I was too scared to write anything remotely close to my life. I thought it would mess up my story as well, like it had messed up my marriage and my career. I didn't want my life story—those twisted beliefs—to jinx my writing. Hence, I purposely stayed away from my life experiences, and from the truth.

But what's the point of writing pages after pages that's devoid of any true feeling? Isn't writing an expression of our emotions? Then how could I be truthful to my readers if I wasn't being honest with myself?

I was back to square one again. A blank page and a blinking cursor laughed at me and mocked my inability. Failure was, indeed, hard to swallow; I hadn't tasted that bitter pill in a long time, not since I had left my school hallway in Goa with a disappointing final-year report card.

Maybe my writing days were behind me. Should I do more columns in investment magazines or go back to my old job? But wouldn't that be a step backward? Adeline's face came to mind. After all, I had already promised her that I wouldn't give up until I had tried everything for the next six months. I owed it to her, and I owed it to myself.

Time is also a funny thing: it moves quickly when you're too busy to look at it, but it refuses to move when you stare it in the eye. While most days we all complain about not having enough time, try spending one full day looking at a clock, second by second, and you'll know what I mean. And with no real progress in my writing, my time started moving at that snail's pace.

The one thing looking up for me was the approaching Christmas holiday; I was supposed to return to Singapore to spend time with Matthew and Lisa. I reached Singapore a day earlier than planned, and as I pressed the doorbell to surprise them all, I noticed the old birdcage on the front porch. The cage door was half-open and there was a small bowl with bird food and a pot of water inside. I was surprised that Mimi had really meant what she said that day.

Mimi answered the door. I was still looking at the cage. I said, "I noticed you kept the cage door open."

"Some birds don't like to live in a cage; so it's better to let them fly back and forth," she answered.

I smiled.

Meanwhile, Matthew and Lisa came running, and hugged me tight – Matthew first, and soon Lisa jumped on top of him. They quickly dragged me into the living room to see their Christmas tree. I immediately succumbed to the love and warmth inside. I was glad I came early.

No doubt my time passed more quickly there in Singapore; but why couldn't I feel happy about that?

Something was pricking my conscience, and I wondered if by any chance I was avoiding facing myself and the blank screen at Phuket. I had promised Adeline six months of work, not just idling away my time. I needed to come face-to-face with my fears; so two days later, I decided to see my old psychiatrist, Dr. Peter Tai, to get some answers.

His office was in a stylish modern building in town; inside it was perfectly harmonized with upscale drapes and leather furniture. A pretty receptionist at the front desk greeted me; though I didn't remember her name, she apparently remembered mine. "Dr. Tai will see you now, Mr. Fernandez." Knowing I had spoken with Dr. Tai earlier that day, she immediately ushered me to his room.

Dr. Tai looked a little puzzled as I entered his office, and asked me whether I was okay.

I said, "I'm fine. How are you doing, Dr. Tai?"

"Oh, I'm good. You look a little different, though."

"Different how?"

"I don't know yet. Tell me what's going on in your life."

I told Dr. Tai everything: why I had left my job, and what I wanted to do. I also told him about my fear of failure.

I tried to summarize the problems for him. "In my head I can do a lot of things; but in actual fact, nothing I do come up to the mark. I know I'm not a genius, but I also know that I'm not stupid either—and that makes me an average guy, whom I'm struggling to live with. It's an excruciating pain, with no immediate danger to one's life, but slowly it cripples one to death. No, I'm not nearly as fearful of death as much as living life in a meaningless way."

It felt good, being able to release all my frustrations. Of course, we can't go tell our friends things like this without being judged; I also knew that I couldn't talk to my walls in Phuket. But I guess it's always different with a shrink.

Leaning back on his dark leather sofa, he replied, "Define average for me, Rohan. By my definition, you aren't an average guy on the street. For heaven's sake, look at you: you're wearing an Armani jacket, you drive a BMW, and you live in a big house. You call that average? Well, even if you do, so be it. And let me tell you, average is good, average is normal. Most of us are average. Why do you want to be different?"

I didn't know how to explain to him that it wasn't so much about being different for the sake of being different; it was the fear of being useless. It was more about not being able to do something worthwhile in life, and not being able to leave a mark here. How much more average can one get? I tried to substantiate my argument, but nothing solid came out at first to back me up; I murmured, "I didn't mean that."

"Remember, you told me once that you're a very average student in school?" asked Dr. Tai.

"So?"

"Tell me what made you change your mind in Singapore. Why did you suddenly decide to study hard in college here?"

"I don't know," was my exasperated answer.

"The point is that it's the average people who often perform above-average acts. All they need is an impetus—a thrust. Were you ever jealous of your sister, Rita?"

"I don't know, maybe a little, but I guess, more pissed off than anything else. When we were in school, she was such a star student; her perfect scores always made me look bad. I wished I could do better."

"You're right, Rohan; what you felt toward her that motivated you to improve yourself to become more like her."

Well, there might have been some truth in that. She was smart and intelligent. Had I secretly made her my role model? I closed my eyes and tried to remember.

But Dr. Tai interrupted me. "And then, what about Mimi?"

"What about her?"

"Did you ever resent her wealth or her parents having more money than you had?"

"Well, maybe a tiny bit. There were times I felt I had to do better to prove myself to her and to her family. And maybe that's how I was dragged into that circus. Anyway, what has all that got to do with my present situation?"

Dr. Tai leaned forward and looked me in the eye. "It shows that you actually do better in a competitive environment. In your childhood, you always aspired to be like your sister; it could've been a family-induced environmental effect, but when you met Mimi you set new goals, and she became your new role model and motivation. Your childhood goals soon changed to earning more money."

"But money and success aren't the same thing, right?"

"Maybe; maybe not. It depends on the time and place; it depends on the yardstick you are measuring success with; it depends on who you are and what you want in life."

Suddenly Mr. Barco's voice echoed in my head: "Most often we don't know what we want from life." True enough; how could I measure my own success if didn't know what I really wanted?

Dr. Tai paused for a moment and then continued. "Let's first understand what success is. Many see it as a series of achievements all stacked up. But success comes in many shapes and sizes. To a film star, it may be an Oscar; to a tennis player, it may be the Wimbledon; to a writer, maybe the Booker Prize; and to a heart surgeon it may be saving a precious life. While being able to run one hundred meters at the fastest speed possible is success to a sprinter, it's sheer stupidity to a marathon runner who needs to hold their energy until much longer. You need to find that yardstick first by which you can measure whether you're successful or not. And don't forget that your goals also change over time.

"When you first came to Singapore, you tried to succeed in school; and I have a feeling your yardstick for success became money after you met Mimi. In other words, you changed your benchmark for success, and you got what you wanted. You've a good career, great family, and a sound financial disposition."

I cut him off abruptly. "I know all that, Dr. Tai. Truly, I know. But what if I want to measure my success with a yardstick above all these—my career, money, and my family? I know the sun and the moon will rise even after we're gone, the mountains will continue to delight everyone, and the waves will still come crashing down the beach. But how do all these things connect each of us with the universe? And when I find the answer, I want that to be my yardstick for success. My old teacher, Mr. Barco, told me that we're bound to leave our fingerprints here—one way or another. I want to know how, and I want to know what my fingerprints will do to the world."

And in that moment of excitement, I suddenly found clarity—I found my own cure. I stood up and walked to the door and said, "Well, thanks, Dr. Tai."

Chapter 20

I RETURNED TO PHUKET the next morning. I hadn't quite found the answer to what I was looking for; but I thought I finally knew the way there. While talking with Dr. Tai, it had suddenly dawned on me that during all this time, my heart wanted to find a purpose in my life and my mind wanted to write a novel. Therefore, the more I tried to concentrate on my writing, the further I was driven from my search. But both needed my undivided attention.

However, Mr. Barco had told me, "In life, you don't always have to choose one or the other; even two contradictory elements can coexist. Although we're more used to seeing the sun during the day, occasionally we can also see the moon in the daylight, while the sun is blazing through the western sky. And other times, even when we can't see them together, they're still there."

That got me thinking. Could my novel work like a big mirror, detailing my search much like the way the moon reflects back the sun's light? Indeed, what better way to write my novel than to link it to my search for the truth? What better way to find the truth than to focus on the search itself? Knowing the ultimate connection with eternity was definitely my new yardstick for success; and documenting that search could easily leave my fingerprints here.

Could that search be my muse? I could certainly write a story about a young man who, after experiencing a volcanic eruption in his mind, leaves home and family in search of the ultimate truth in life. That way my two vital issues would no longer be two competing forces, but could complement each other. Besides, what could be more intriguing than a true story?

I had been wasting time looking for characters and materials for my book, not knowing that the best material was lying right under my nose all this time. Now I understood from my earlier mistakes that truth and honesty in writing would also go a long way.

I was convinced that now I could be in any place—Andaman or Alaska, Pasadena or Phuket, it would all be the same, just a backdrop as my inward journey took center stage. My mind was finally aligned with my writing. My writing was aligned with my search. My search was aligned with my goal. I was truly ready. I was also ready to take on the questions that I had been avoiding all this while.

As my mind settled down, I realized that to remain committed and to be totally truthful, I had to get hold of my inner self, the part of me that occasionally showed glimpses of light, once in a while whispered in my ears all the wonders of the world, and at the same time made my life a living hell with all the difficult questions no one ever wanted to answer. But where was my soul? I didn't even notice that it'd gone missing; how could I find it again?

What do we do when we face a major crisis? We usually go to the roots; we go to the origin to find the source of the problem. When an epidemic breaks out, we may go look for the cure first; but in order to eradicate the disease, we still need to find the source of that virus and take action accordingly. Similarly, what do we do when we lose something or someone precious to us? We go to the place where that something or someone was last seen, and from there we work out other probabilities.

The next morning when I woke up, I knew exactly what I had to do. My soul had been detached from the rest of my body a long time ago, like a train delinks a few cars at a certain destination and proceeds with the rest of the passengers willing to travel farther.

I couldn't deny that I had changed since I had left Goa after high school; maybe it was too much of a change for my soul to cope with. When situations become intense, we all do the same: leave to avoid confrontation. I had left my family and my office for the same reason, so I guess I couldn't blame my soul for abandoning me. All I could do was find it again and beg for forgiveness.

I packed my bag and left Phuket to go search for my soul—to start from where I started—where I had last come face-to-face with my inner self.

I arrived at the airport in forty-five minutes, bought a ticket, and within hours I was on the way to my hometown in Goa. As we took off and vanished into the clouds, I realized why people keep saying, 'Life is a journey, not a destination.' Everything about life is about this moment in time. Chances are, if we aren't happy with our journey, we'll never be happy with the destination. Most of us are perpetually waiting; we leave home waiting to reach the airport, but after arriving at the airport we wait for the plane to leave. Then after takeoff we can't wait to reach the destination. Unfortunately, the waiting doesn't end even after reaching the destination. There we wait for the activities to begin, or to go out and so on, and finally we can't wait to come back home.

This time, for a change, I wasn't waiting for touchdown; I was in no hurry. I wanted to hold on to and savor every moment. Life is magical the moment we open our eyes. But how many times in life do we get to enjoy that experience? More often than not we live our lives blindfolded—figuratively, of course. How often do we take time to look at the morning dew in our own backyards, or blow bubbles with our kids, drench ourselves silly in the rain, and whisper, 'I love you' under starry nights? Like it or not, we all seem to like the rat race more than the rats do; we hardly notice the important things in life even when our eyes are open.

It was blue sky outside with fragments of white clouds. How many times in my life had I actually noticed the earth from 38,000 feet? With sharp eyes one could see the tiny houses below. I had flown several times in my life, but never had the time or mental makeup to enjoy the ride. Now I had the perfect opportunity to do that. The clouds were playing hide and seek underneath the airplane belly. I put my headphones on to jazz it up with music. There was a real party going on in my head.

My flight landed at a quarter after eleven in the morning, and one hour later, the cab pulled up in front of my mom's house. My mother was sitting on a chair on the front balcony, waiting for my arrival. She looked a little pale, but I didn't mention anything. I hadn't seen my mother for close to four or five months. I felt excited; after all, coming home always had a different feeling, and especially this time.

"Hi, Mom! How're you doing?"

Even after helping my mother relocate here, I had asked her several times to come visit me in Phuket, but she always said, "You know what, I may be alone, but I'm not lonely. With age we lose many of our activities and most of our friends, but we always have our best friend with us: memory. And that gives us company; that keeps us going. Old age is about memories. Life then revolves around your past. Once I close my eyes I can see everything. This is my home, and I want to live here."

Looking around the house carefully, I understood what she had meant. The pictures on the wall wasn't the only thing with stories to tell; each corner was filled with memories, and each molecule and atom in that house breathed life. The corner of the wall that had been chipped when I dragged my bicycle into my room, the height scale my sister drew on the wall to keep track of how tall I grew every month, the big globe across the hall we used to kick around, and a few tiny medals I received in story-writing competitions—in spite of the renovations - my mother had preserved it all so carefully that I could almost touch those memories.

Right after lunch, I pulled another chair next to my mother's rocking chair on the rear balcony. Everything looked absolutely peaceful, heavenly. We sat side by side for hours and said nothing, yet I could feel her warmth. Communication between two people isn't necessarily at its best only when they talk, it can also reach a new high in total silence.

I heard the sound of the waves, took in the pungent smell of the sea, and closed my eyes. My mind traveled back in time when I was a young child and my old memories kept flashing in and out: I could clearly see my grandma rocking next to me, and at a distance few boys and girls playing beach volleyball and yelling at each other, and fishermen trying hard to keep their dinghy boats under control in the middle of the sea.

Suddenly, the wind blew my baseball cap away; I opened my eyes and saw the present version of myself sitting in that chair. Everything still looked the same. The wind was as strong as it used to be in the summer days of my childhood. Some new kids were playing beach volleyball at a distance, and fishermen were still struggling to keep their boats afloat with their catch of the day. The changes we think or talk about are all at micro levels. My mother had taken over my grandma's rocking chair; but when I considered this as a part of a bigger picture, I recognized that one old lady had replaced another old lady, like the kids playing on the beach or the fishermen out in the sea today weren't the same people I had seen twenty years before, but the scene was all the same.

So, what does that tell us? Does it mean that our birth or death don't make any difference in the universe? Does it mean that we don't have much value as an individual? Are we only just one part of a big scene? Or does this mean, like Ade's jigsaw puzzle, god also has one big puzzle of his own, where we form one piece each; and he is trying to fit us all in that big picture?

Even then, each piece in a jigsaw puzzle is as important as the whole puzzle, because if we lose one piece we can't complete that puzzle anymore. So, as Mr. Barco said, everyone still has an opportunity to create their own identification mark.

Each person is unique on their own; and this uniqueness makes them as essential as any small piece in a jigsaw puzzle. I realized there's an inherent link between one and all, because essentially there's no all without one.

I pushed my chair back slightly to avoid the direct sunlight falling on my eyes; it was starting to bother me. Yet, I didn't want to go inside and miss out on one of the most captivating parts of Goa's scenic beauty.

Indeed, the sunset in Goa is incredible. The sun doesn't hide behind another building or rows of trees; because Goa is at the western tip of India, on a clear day one can see the sun dropping into the middle of the Arabian Sea. And the western sky becomes a rogue painter's canvas with no rules, no limitations; the choice of colors and materials are all up to the creator and him alone. To many it might seem meaningless to watch the sky for an hour or two— at times, even longer; but those who love this kind of wild painting, when nature throws colors at whim, stay breathless till the sun sets and the residues are all gone. These folks know that even the best photographers in the world dare not say they and their cameras can do justice to that moment of time. The best one can do, I guess, is to take it all in and preserve that moment in the mind for eternity.

I was sure my mother had been doing that religiously since she had come back to Goa, and she wanted me to soak myself in that feeling as well. When I volunteered to help her make coffee, she ordered me to stay put and enjoy the sunset instead. She knew me so well. Although she had never interfered with anything in my whole life, I didn't want to keep her in the dark about my visit anymore. I told her that I had left my job and wanted to start writing.

"That's a great idea, Rohan. I believe you can do that."

"You think so?"

"No, Rohan, I don't think so; I know so. As much as we all need our eyes to see things, the actual seeing starts after we close our eyes. Doesn't it? Write not about what you see; write how your mind interprets what you see."

I'd always had a thinking mind. When I was young, I didn't have many friends; but I didn't feel the lack of it, because my thoughts would occupy my mind the whole time. In fact, that was my private arena, my place for comfort, my pride. My thoughts were like my best friends. I didn't care much about money or fame; but I did care about my thoughts. They were my only possessions; they were my identity. But I wasn't so sure about one thing, so I asked, "Who would ever want to read my thoughts?"

"I don't think that should be your concern now. First, people who write do so because they love to write. Secondly, as you know, each life is different; so are each person's ideas. If you're being honest in writing your own thoughts, I'm sure they'll be as original as yourself. And any original thought has its value in history. If all that means more people reading and more books selling, that's a bonus."

The sun was about to set on the horizon; it almost touched the Arabian Sea, and the sky was painted with hues of orange and red.

I couldn't stop admiring the incredible gifts of nature we all get to experience all day, every day, anywhere, and everywhere. One thing still holds true: we all hold equal rights to the sunlight, the moonlight, the balmy summer breeze, the magic of fall, and the wonders of winter. Then why do we go searching for life anywhere else when it is all right here within our grasp—in our own neighborhood, living and breathing next to us?

What had happened to me all these years? Where did I go, and why? Maybe all I did was traveling on a giant Ferris wheel or jumping higher and higher on a trampoline in my own backyard, because every time I was brought right back from where I had started. Isn't coming back a law of nature? I remembered what Mr. Barco had told his brother in

Lauterbrunnen: "The day and the night come back, the months come back, the leaves come back; everything in nature is a continuous process." I also realized now that there's no beginning and there's no end in life. It's not about starting or finishing; it's about collecting experiences along the way. At a micro level, maybe we all go from one school to another in search of a better education, we go from one place to another in search of new job opportunities, and after spending our stipulated time here, we pass the baton to the next person much like in a relay race; but at a macro level, it's just another process in nature—nothing personal.

Who knows, maybe I'm just another link in a huge chain in the universe. Individually, there may be an end to everything, and there may be an end to every person, but collectively everything lasts forever. When one runner passes the baton to the next runner in a relay race, that person's job maybe over, but collectively the race goes on. Like the day my dad retired, Mr. Chen, the assistant principal gladly took over all his school responsibilities to continue the school legacy. Likewise, a science research also doesn't stop when its lead scientist passes away; a new scientist steps in to start from where his predecessor had left off. As much as individual performance is important, it's the collective performance that takes the relay team to the victory stand. But let's not forget that all links in a chain revolve and circle back to their previous position again and again. Yes, of course, each link is important, but collectively the chain is thousand times more important, because it keeps the whole process moving.

The sky was beginning to get dark. I noticed a long, straight line of ants crawling past the balcony railing, exactly as I had often seen them when I was a young boy. I slowly got up from my chair, stood close to the line of ants, stooped a little, and watched them crawling one after another; they all marched forward in a never-ending procession. They had no time to waste; each one had to do its part to keep this gigantic line moving. As one ant moved forward, another took its position, like a chain made of a zillion links. Each link had a time span and a purpose: to connect the previous link to the next.

Had Mr. Barco meant something like this when he talked about leaving our mark here? Sooner or later each ant would die, and so would I, someday. But each one of us, whether rich and successful or poor and desolate, leaves behind the legacy of connecting one link to the next to continue the push to the cycle of eternity.

More books from Harvard Square Editions

Augments of Change, Kelvin Christopher James

Gates of Eden, Charles Degelman

Love's Affliction, Fidelis Mkparu

Transoceanic Lights, S. Li

Close, Erika Raskin

Anomie, Jeff Lockwood

Living Treasures, Yang Huang

A Face in the Sky, Greg Jenkins

Nature's Confession, J.L. Morin

Dark Lady of Hollywood, Diane Haithman

Fugue for the Right Hand, Michele Tolela Myers

Growing Up White, James P. Stobaugh

The Beard, Alan Swyer

Parallel, Sharon Erby

www.ingramcontent.com/pod-product-compliance
Lightning Source LLC
Chambersburg PA
CBHW031957010726
47493CB00007B/2237